COMING HOME

COMING HOME

Wolves of Collier Pack

By

Julie Trettel

Coming Home
Wolves of Collier Pack: Book Five

Cover Art by, Bridgette O'Hare of Dark Unicorn Designs
Editing by, Sara Meadows of TripleA Publishing Services

Thanks and Acknowledgments

This book was very near and dear to my heart as an Army brat and mother of a stillborn. So it is only fitting this book is dedicated to all the men and women serving or who have served in the United States Military. Many blessings to you and your families for the sacrifice you give each and every day.

A special shout out to Rachel (National Guard). I know you're going to do amazing things with your life! I'm so proud of you!!!

I'd also like to dedicate this book to all the silent babies born too soon, and the mothers and fathers of empty arms. God bless each of you.

In memory of Taylor Marie Trettel, born still June 10, 1998.

Shelby

Chapter 1

There are two types of small-town girls in this world: the ones who can't wait to get out and see the world, and those of us who simply want to find our one true mate and settle down to start a family. I always knew I'd be the latter, but much to my disappointment, that did not happen.

Today I was turning twenty-seven. By the time, I was twenty I'd already started getting "those" comments, as if I were an old maid or something

"Shelby, what are you going to do with your future?"

"Shelby, you can't just sit around waiting for someone who might never come."

"Shelby, you have to do something with your life."

I had skirted through every basic job in our territory and I hated them all. I wanted to be a mom. I didn't want to leave Collier, but I knew I'd make a hell of a great Pack Mother if that were my destiny. By this point in my life, I'd given up hope that either would ever happen for me.

I knew some of my sisters had been much older when they first found their mates, but Dad wasn't going to just let me sit around doing nothing while I waited for mine.

Two summers ago, I started working in the Collier youth center and it had really opened my eyes to a potential career. After I graduated high school, Dad had insisted I needed a college education. I hadn't gone away to school like Lizzy and Clara, but I had found an online program that appeased him and had even graduated. Turned out it wasn't too hard to go back and get my teaching certificate because of that. It wasn't a career I'd ever considered before, but two weeks ago it became my new life.

I was now Ms. Shelby, English teacher at Collier Middle School. Most people assumed those junior high years were the absolute worst age to work with. It was often a tough time for kids, but I'd personally loved that age in my life and already knew from working with the after-school program at the center last year that I most enjoyed working with the kids that age in my Pack.

For me, growing up had been easy. Why? Because I'd always had Ben by my side.

Benjamin Shay and I had been best friends since we were in diapers. We grew up doing everything together. Literally every great story of my life started with "Ben and I . . ."

He was there when I fell out of a tree and broke my arm when we were six. He'd insisted on carrying me the entire way home, despite the fact my legs worked just fine.

By age ten he began getting teased for hanging out with a girl all the time. Ben had never cared about that and told them they'd all be jealous someday. He was right: by seventh grade, the boys started noticing me and that's when everyone wanted to be Ben's friend.

Grayson Ward was my first boyfriend, in eighth grade. When I confided in Ben one day down by the river that I was nervous about getting my first kiss at a party the next weekend that Grayson and I were going to, Ben sat me down on a boulder and told me not to worry.

"I'm not going to let Grayson ruin your first kiss, sport," he said, seconds before his lips touched mine.

I had been momentarily stunned and just sat there frozen, but he had kept kissing me until I relaxed. When I sighed, my mouth had opened just a little and he'd stuck his tongue in. It was a crazy sensation at the time. I had never kissed a boy before, let alone French kissed one, but Ben was patient and a really good kisser, though I didn't know that until the next weekend when Grayson had laid one on me and aggressively tried French kissing. I nearly gagged and we broke up the next day.

Everyone assumed things between us would change in high school, but they never did. I taught him how to dance before prom. He taught me to drive. We did everything together and were inseparable.

Basically, Ben had been my first everything in life, and then he just disappeared. Without any warning whatsoever, and one month to the day after the greatest night of my life, my best friend and the only man I had ever loved walked out of my life with barely a goodbye.

The night before he left, he showed up at my house asking if I could go for a drive. He broke the news then that he had enlisted into the army and was going out for the Ranger's program. I didn't understand how that would work, knowing he could never shift and let his wolf out with so many people constantly watching him, but he assured me it would be fine.

I cried when he hugged me goodbye without even a final kiss and walked away. Of course, at the time I thought it was only temporary. He'd go off to boot camp and I'd fly out to meet him before he started his next training. I was prepared to wait for him, and I wrote to him every single day. The first few weeks I had heard from him, but by the end of boot camp letters from Ben were rare.

He made an excuse as to why I couldn't fly out to see him for graduation. I accepted that, and continued to write him, every single day. He wrote to me for the last time four months later, telling me he was being deployed.

I never personally heard from him again after that. I still wrote to him every day for two years straight. It wasn't until I found out, after the fact, that his parents and younger brothers had flown out to visit with him, that I finally stopped sending the letters.

He hadn't called or asked me to join them. Clearly, he had moved on, and it hurt. Heck, it still hurt. Everyone told me to let him go, but I couldn't. Peyton was the only one that knew I still wrote to him every single day since. I just no longer mailed the letters. They went into a box on the top shelf of my closet.

Ben's mother still kept me updated on where he was and how he was doing. She was so proud of him and I never let on how much it hurt to hear her stories. I knew he had been shot the previous year, and still he had refused to come home. He never thought to call and tell me he was at least alive. He didn't need me anymore. That much was obvious. Some days it made me so angry. He may have gotten his closure easily enough, but I still hadn't, and every time I even attempted to go on a date or move past it, inevitably I compared them all to Ben, and no man had ever been able to live up to that bar he had set.

The bell rang, jolting me back to the present and away from the bittersweet memories that would probably always haunt me. My last class of the day began to wander in, seventh grade English. I equally loved and dreaded this class every day, mostly because Ben's twin little brothers were in it.

Troy and Will were a constant reminder of what was missing in my life. I loved those boys so much. They had only been in preschool when their brother left and I had tried to be there for them for the first few years, but then it just became so hard. When I stopped sending the letters, I stopped visiting the boys, too. But fate has a way of bringing things full circle—or just laughing in my face—because now I was stuck with them every day.

Troy looked so much like Ben at this age, and Will had no clue just how much like Ben he acted, right down to his best friend, Caroline Wilson. It was hard watching the two of them, and some days I just wanted to shake little Caroline and yell, "Don't fall for it the way I did. Those Shay boys are nothing but heartbreakers!"

"Ms. Shelby?" Troy said as he walked up to my desk.

"Yes, Troy?"

"I heard a rumor that some of the Larken wolves were going to be joining our school this year. Is that true?"

I sighed. Rumors spread quickly in a small town.

"I've heard that as well, but I don't have any real confirmation that it's true."

Will rolled his eyes when he walked up to my desk to stand next to his twin. They didn't look alike, but together, they were like a mini Ben.

"You're the Alpha's sister, Ms. Shelby. Of course you know," Will challenged.

I smirked. In truth, I didn't. I hadn't wanted to ask Thomas. I figured if he wanted me to know, he'd tell me, and since he hadn't, I suspected it was still just a rumor, probably with a little truth, like maybe he and Luke Larken, Alpha of the Larken wolves, were discussing it.

"Actually, Will, I don't. I'll let you guys know if I do, but so far Thomas really hasn't mentioned anything to me about it."

My sister Peyton had mated a Larken wolf and since then Thomas and Luke had been discussing a lot of things. The Larken wolves used to be part of Collier Pack until Jedidiah Larken had a falling out with my dad and left the Pack, taking several families with him. Unfortunately, he wasn't a very good leader and left them destitute and struggling in a rundown trailer park with no land to run on.

Most of the Larken wolves were into drugs, alcohol, sex, and riding fast motorcycles. The local humans considered them a dangerous biker gang. There was a little truth in that. I asked Peyton's mate, Oliver, about it once, and he told me that while the rush was not comparable, it was the next best thing to shifting, which was dangerous for them to do.

The Larken Pack now ran once a month with Peyton and Oliver on the land they had bought just outside Collier, in neutral territory. There were talks about merging the packs back, but so far that hadn't happened. Thomas did hire a lot of the Larken wolves after one of the big factories in town closed and so far there hadn't been any major issues from it. Rumors of their kids coming to Collier schools started surfacing shortly after that.

"Come on, Shelby, you have to tell us," Troy whined.

"Troy, we talked about this. It's Ms. Shelby at school or Ms. Collier even, but it's a rule and we need to follow it," I reminded him.

"But you will tell us if you hear anything for sure?" Will asked.

"Yes, I promise. Now take your seats and let's get this class started."

The class time passed quickly. They really were just a great group of kids. I wasn't as strict as some of the other more seasoned teachers, but since I'd been working with them for a few years at the youth center, I had already gained their respect and the transition so far had been a seamless one.

When the bell finally rang, I watched my students get up and scurry for the door.

"Don't forget you have a paper due on Monday. Have a great weekend," I hollered after them.

Teaching was an exhausting, sometimes thankless job, but I was loving it. Watching Troy and Will leave my classroom, I was struck again by their uncanny similarities to their brother.

I didn't want to think about him, but my mind wandered to that place so easily. I couldn't help but think of what he might be doing and where Ben was right at that moment.

Ben

Chapter 2

"Shay, get your ass over here."

"Yes, Major!" I retorted. "Sir, what can I do for you, sir?"

Major Collins looked up from his desk and laughed.

"At ease, Sergeant. Heard you had some issues in the field today. What's up?"

I sighed and scrubbed my face with both my hands. "May I speak candidly, sir?"

"Take a seat, no need for formalities, Ben. Now what's going on?"

"These new recruits suck, Jeff. There's no way they are going to cut it. I'm tired of being benched. I miss my team. Send me back into the field. Just sign the paperwork, please. Overseeing these guys is worse than the desk job you had me assigned to, and I have to ride around in this stupid wheelchair looking weak and pathetic. I'm not either," I insisted.

"Ben, you were shot in the spine. Physicians checked you over, it was documented. This is the second major injury you've had."

"I'm fine, and we both know it," I argued.

"I know this, you know this, but neither of us can afford for them to know this. You think it's easy to hide this division in plain sight in the United States Army? Well, it's not. If I sign off on release forms only two weeks after an injury you weren't supposed to walk away from, we're going to get investigated."

"Fine, then document it however you feel is necessary and send me back in. As long as it looks right on paper, no one will even know I'm gone, and you know that's true."

"You've been a pain in my ass for the last nine years, you know that?"

I laughed. "Yeah, you don't let me forget it."

"I inherited this command because those in the know knew I could handle it and be discreet about the slightly less-than-human soldiers running about. Shifters were discovered on the war front back in World War II. Eyewitnesses say they were saved by various animals that appeared out of nowhere amongst the smoke and flames. Other reports said there was a batch of either zombies or vampires that rose from the ashes after having been shot dead."

"It's not impossible to shoot and kill us, but we do heal quickly, so if it's not a perfect kill shot, it just hurts like a son-of-a-bitch and takes a couple days to recover. Or, as you know, a quick shift and I was good to go within twenty-four hours. It nicked my spine at most. This isn't a big deal."

"That's because you're not human."

"Exactly," I argued.

"And that's exactly what I'm trying to do, to save your ass from others finding out."

We'd been having the same argument for days.

"Look, I called you in here to tell you that I've requested a doctor to verify your progress. He's one of my guys, human, but he'll keep his mouth shut about your miraculous recovery. He's seen others walk away from worse in this unit. On paper he's going to find you safe to move and recommend you rejoin your unit due to depression."

"Aww, man, not depression. They'll assign me a damn shrink," I grumbled.

"That's the best that I can do, Ben. At least you'll be back with the boys and if you happen to sneak out during that time and join the team, well, let's just say heads will roll if any of you are stupid enough to put that in a report. You were never there, are we clear?"

"Crystal. And for the record, shifters have been battling in wars alongside humans from a lot longer than World War II." I grinned when he rolled his eyes.

Finally, I was getting sprung from this hellhole.

"There is one final thing, though. He's not coming until tomorrow, and you're taking one of the new recruits back with you. So, I can pick him, or you can. You've been working with these guys for the last two weeks. I trust you. You know better than anyone who and what we need on the team," the major said.

I rolled my eyes. "I'm stuck with one of these morons?"

"Officially, he'll be your temporary replacement."

"What?"

"Shay, I have to do this so it looks like you're a normal human recovering at least on paper. You know this. I'm not going to sit here and keep repeating myself. You have until tomorrow morning to decide, or I will do it for you."

"Yes, sir," I said as I turned my chair around and wheeled towards the door.

"And do me a favor and take a close look at Jake today," he said as I was about to exit.

I sighed and nodded without even bothering to turn around. Jeff had made up his mind and that was his passive-aggressive way of letting me know. Of all the people Jake would have been my last pick. I wasn't sure what his animal spirit was, but the kid was cocky and overly confident. I was certain he'd never failed at anything in life and he let everyone know it. It didn't make him much of a team player. Plus, he talked too goddamn much for my taste.

I didn't like the new plan, but if it got me away from this hellhole and back to my team, I'd take it. I hated this wheelchair more than I could possibly say in words. It wasn't even a regular one, but a damn electric chair, because with my spinal injury, I wasn't supposed to have full use of my arms yet, just enough to operate the stick on the arm of the thing.

The depression thing wasn't entirely off base, and I knew I would feel better just being around the guys. I hated being separated from them. Someone had to cover their asses, and that someone was me.

Plus, anytime I had too much downtime on my hands, my mind wandered back to a period in my life that would likely haunt me until the day I died. I knew I had done the right thing in leaving, but that didn't mean it didn't feel like a part of me had been severed in the process.

No matter what I did or how I tried to rid myself of the memories of her, nothing ever worked. Staying busy was the only thing that kept me from going crazy. And these last two weeks, I hadn't had much work to do. I tried not to even think her name. *Shelby Collier*. I sighed, trying to push my demons back into place.

She was the one thing I had never shared with my brothers in arms. They knew I still carried a stack of letters from her on me at every mission. We weren't supposed to ever bring something so personal on a mission, but I had blown up enough times over the years about it that the guys just looked the other way.

I knew they all assumed she was dead. It was easier than the truth, so I let them believe it. She had written every day for the first two years, then she finally stopped. Never once did she mention him in any of them. She'd hinted about something important she needed to tell me when I was still in boot camp, but she hadn't, and I'd asked her not to come out with my parents on graduation day. In some ways, that had been even harder than telling her I had joined the army.

Shelby had been my best friend my entire life. There was nothing I wouldn't do for that girl. She was mine and I had always imagined we'd grow up, mate, have a few pups, and live happily ever after. It didn't matter if we were true mates or not, because as best friends and lovers, we were already as close as that.

Shelby's wolf came in first, just two weeks before graduation. Four days later Grayson Ward approached me and explained that his wolf was mated to Shelby's. We'd never discussed what would happen if one of us found our true mate; heck, Shelby and I had never discussed a future together. I just always assumed. I've never again assumed anything in life.

I had tried to talk to her about it, but she was acting weird, not herself at all, and I knew she was struggling to tell me. We argued one night, and I'd asked her point blank if it was because of him. I thought back to that night.

"Sport, what's wrong? You're not acting like yourself." I had been genuinely worried about her and still upset, trying to deal with the idea of her and Grayson together.

Shelby had lost her virginity to me at prom just a few weeks earlier. I honestly thought that was the start of our future and I was excited about it. I'd get a full-time job out at the ranch and as soon as I could afford it, I'd buy us a house and take her officially as my mate. But Grayson had destroyed that vision and I was still too stubborn to believe it.

"I don't know, Ben. It's just these weird feelings I'm having. I can't even put them into words yet. I just feel off, incomplete with myself, I guess," she said.

I knew that was her way of telling me about Grayson. Shelby hated direct conflict. I understood her well enough to see the picture clearly. It was all true.

I'd tried to coax it out of her. I even asked her point blank if it had to do with Grayson Ward, and she'd gotten angrier than I'd ever remembered seeing her before.

"I told you, I don't know what the hell is happening!" she had yelled, then stormed away.

The next day at school things between us were a little strained, but she packed my favorite lunch of her mother's famous meatloaf dinner and apologized. That was another thing Shelby Collier rarely ever did.

I was ready to forgive her. After much thought I had decided that no matter what, I still wanted Shelby in my life. That only lasted until the end of the school day. I swung by her classroom to see if she wanted to go get milkshakes when I went to pick up some stuff for my mom in town.

Collier had a lot of great things, but bread to my mother's satisfaction wasn't one of them. She always made it from scratch. My mouth watered now just thinking about it. But anyway, there was a specific brand of organic flour she preferred to use, and the Collier grocery didn't carry it. She asked me to pick some up for her and of course, I'd said yes.

After the final bell rang, I headed for the hallway Shelby's last class was on. As I rounded the corner, I skidded to a halt. She and Grayson were standing outside her classroom. He placed a possessive hand on her arm and leaned in to whisper something. With all the excess noise around me as students made their final locker deposits and proceeded to leave for the day, I couldn't hear what he said, even with my new advanced wolf hearing that was just beginning to come in.

Shelby threw her head back and laughed. As Grayson pulled back from her, he caught my eye, grinned, and nodded. Then he had the audacity to wink at me and I saw red. I had never wanted to punch anyone in the face as badly as I wanted to hit Grayson. Seeing red and not wanting to make a scene, I turned and left.

I don't even remember the drive over to the next town, or how my mom's items ended up in the backseat of my car. I was in a haze, parked outside the ice cream shop I had wanted to bring Shelby to. I got out of the car, but couldn't bring myself to go in. Shelby had always loved going there.

Instead, I'd found myself walking into the store next to it—only it wasn't a store, it was a recruitment center, and a few hours later I drove home to break the news to my parents that I'd just signed my life away to the United States Army.

Mom cried. So did the twins. Dad kept repeating, "What have you done?" He thought it was impulsive and dangerous. He questioned what would happen when my wolf came in. It didn't matter. Somehow, I'd make it work. I had to, because once you signed that dotted line, you'd written your name in blood, sweat, and years, and there was no backing out.

By the next day it was like I suddenly had my girl back. She acted as if everything was perfectly fine, but I knew the truth and it would never be fine again.

I waited until the night before I left to tell her what I'd done. She'd cried, then pulled herself together and told me it was going to all be okay. She told me she'd still be here waiting, always. She said I should go and fulfill my obligations and do what I felt I needed to do, and then come home. And when I got to the center the next morning after saying goodbye to my family at home, Shelby was there and waiting.

She had tears in her eyes but told me she was proud of me, and that she'd see me in eight weeks at graduation. Then she hugged me, as if everything was perfectly fine.

Three days into boot camp and we were dropped off into the woods with coordinates to get back, but not before surviving a night outdoors with only our standard packs on our back.

They had told us what to carry at all times, drilled it into us even, but it was summer, and it was hot. Most of the guys assigned with me hadn't listened and chose to lighten their load in the heat and take their chances. First, we got lost; then, when we finally stopped arguing enough to pick a campsite, it was dark, and the reality hit us that I was the only person to actually listen. Some had no food, others no shelter. No one thought fire was all that important because they even ditched their matches. I mean, seriously, how much weight does a pack of matches really add?

I was on edge and irritable, snapping at everyone even while I was the one looking out for the dumbasses.

As I lay in my tent, I just couldn't get comfortable. I tossed and turned. It felt like I was lying in an ant hill and they were crawling all over me. I scooted out of my tent and jumped to my feet. I needed to move so I headed deeper into the woods.

"Where are you going?" someone yelled at my retreating back.

"Bathroom," I yelled back.

I did need to do that, too, so it wasn't entirely a lie. When I was done with my business, though, I quickly realized what the problem was. I was shifting for the first time, alone in the woods with humans all around.

I took off as far away as I dared, paying little attention to the direction I was running in. When I felt like I was a safe distance away, I stripped out of my clothes and sat down on the ground to wait. I knew from hearing my friends talk that it could take hours or days.

I sat there with my knees pulled up to my chest, rocking back and forth for what felt like hours, but might have only been minutes. I breathed calmly, trying not to panic. Looking up into the sky, I let my mind wander back to Shelby. I wished she were there with me.

With one sigh and that thought in mind, I shifted for the first time. Unlike many of the horror stories I'd heard over the years, it had been smooth and painless. I even let myself run around a bit and was grateful that by morning light I was back in my skin.

It took me a little while to find my clothes, and then I started heading back on my walk of shame. I didn't know it at the time, but everyone assumed I had gotten lost in the night and a search party was out looking for me.

I had found my way back to camp and retrieved all of my things, even though my unit had abandoned the little they had contributed. As my stomach growled, I realized they had no problems helping themselves to all of my food.

Grumbling, I turned and made my way back to the barracks. Jeff was there evaluating three specific recruits. It was the first time I'd met the man.

"There's an entire squadron out there searching for you, son," he said.

I shrugged. "Sir, sorry, sir. Tripped over a log and twisted my ankle, then I got mixed up on the way back. Waited it out until morning. Those asshats ate all my food."

"One of them called in reports of a wolf in the area. Where there's one wolf there's always more. You're damn lucky."

"Didn't cross paths with anything to be afraid of. Next time I'll remember to bring my flashlight with me when I go for a piss."

I'm not sure what part of that talk triggered Collins on to me, but for the remainder of boot camp I was on his radar. And I had been ever sense.

Now it was Jake's turn to be on radar. I smirked.

"Jake, let's see you run that course again, son," I yelled as I maneuvered my chair towards him at the obstacle course.

He shot me a cocky smile, waved, and took off for another round.

Shelby

Chapter 3

Finally, a completely free weekend! I purposely didn't assign any homework due the second half of the week just so I could have this break. Who knew teaching was so all-consuming? I was still young and in great shape, but those kids wore me out.

We were closing out the first quarter already and testing prep was beginning next week. I needed a little downtime before that started.

The school year was flying by. I was doing a decent job of keeping up with the workload. It sure was a lot worse on this side of school than it was as a student. Boy, did I take so much for granted when I was in their shoes.

I was up early, just like every other day of my life lately. I tried to force myself back to sleep, but it was not happening. I gave up after about half an hour of trying, jumped in the shower, and headed for Kate's Diner. My sister Peyton worked there and made the best breakfast ever.

I parked the car and walked inside.

"Hey, Shelbs. We haven't seen you around here much lately," Kate, the owner, greeted me.

I sighed. "I know. It's not on my way to school and I always seem to be running late."

I heard a laugh behind me. "You were born running late, sweetie."

I turned towards the voice to see my parents already there and seated, and looking much brighter than I felt. My brother Thomas and his mate, Lily, were both there, too.

"What are you guys doing here?" I asked, then yawned.

"Kate, coffee for Shelby, stat," my dad teased.

"I'm on it, sir," she replied good naturedly.

I pulled a chair from a nearby table and sat at the end of their booth.

"I don't recall you being invited to join us," Thomas said with a smirk.

"Bite me," I said under my breath.

"Was she really late to her own birth?" Lily asked, ignoring us both.

"Two weeks past her due date," my mom said.

"And she's never let me live it down," I admitted. "Why is everyone up so early today?"

"Maddie and Liam are arriving this morning, remember," Mom said.

I tried not to groan. No, I didn't remember. I hadn't talked to my youngest sister in over a week. I forgot all about their visit. I instantly felt guilty for feeling disappointed it was this weekend. I just wanted some peace and quiet, and while I loved my niece and nephew to pieces, they came with anything but peace and quiet.

Peyton stepped out of the kitchen to say hello to everyone.

"Hey, Mom, I was wondering if it would be okay with you if Oliver and I host dinner tonight for everyone. I'm only working the morning shift and it would be our first family dinner since we finished the house," Peyton said. I could see she was holding her breath, awaiting Mom's answer.

For good reasons, our mother got very territorial when it came to Maddie. Madelyn had snuck out of the house when she was sixteen to attend a concert with a friend. She'd met some guys and they got her drunk, drugged her, then separated her from her friend.

I shuddered just thinking of her story and everything she went through. Shame and embarrassment kept her away for over eight years before her one true mate crossed paths with her and everything changed. She and Liam were now happily mated and even married. He had adopted Oscar and they gave him a baby sister shortly after. Sara had her big brother wrapped around her little finger.

I was excited to see them. Being a year older, Sara was going to look like a giant next to my other nieces. We didn't see Maddie and Liam as much because they lived in Westin Pack.

Westin got Maddie, and ironically, we got Lily Westin. Now that had been a huge shock to all, and quite humorous. Lily had made it very clear how little she thought of my baby brother, but when she came to Collier as emotional support for Maddie, she'd been in for a huge surprise. Thomas was her true mate, and while he tried to be patient, he made it clear she wasn't getting away.

They had quite the mating period, though not nearly as bad as my oldest sister. Lizzy and Cole had a sad and beautiful story. In some ways I could relate to her, though. She'd met Cole Anderson when they were just teenagers and they both knew they were meant to be together, but she'd stubbornly tried to help the Pack by mating an Alpha heir instead. It hadn't panned out, and her wolf had already begun to bond with Cole. For years they sat in limbo with an unresolved bond. I saw firsthand how that had nearly destroyed her. I vowed not to let the same happen to me.

I sighed and looked down at the cup of coffee that I hadn't even noticed Kate deliver.

I jumped when a sharp pain hit my leg. I looked up and saw Peyton glaring down at me. Shit, I'd lost myself in my own thoughts again. Only Pey really knew about the feelings I still harbored for Ben.

"So six o'clock dinner at my house. Everyone better come. I'm so excited about this. Thanks, Mom," Peyton said. She shot me a glare that told me she was repeating herself for my sake and knew I'd been stuck in my head.

When she headed back to the kitchen, I jumped up and followed her. I grabbed a stool and sat next to the stove, but with enough distance to ensure I didn't get in her way. I knew mornings were crazy in Kate's kitchen, or really, Peyton's kitchen. Hiring my sister to cook was the smartest thing Kate had ever done.

"It's getting worse, you know," she said, not at all surprised to find me shadowing her. "I think it's probably because the twins are in your class and you see his reminders every single day. You have to find a way to control it, Shelbs."

I knew she was just concerned for me. I think she was a little overly sensitive to it after everything Lizzy had gone through.

"I promise you, we never bonded. That's not what this is about. I just feel like a part of me is missing. And I think you're right. Seeing the boys every day is just stirring up all these memories. Will may not be the one that looks like him, but he acts exactly like him, and he's got Caroline who does everything with him. How does that not remind me of us? I can't help it."

"It's been nine years, Shelby. You have other friends. I mean you guys weren't even romantically involved or anything, so it's not like he broke your heart in that way."

I bit my bottom lip and looked out the window. My silence may as well have screamed the truth and one of the biggest secrets I kept from everyone.

"Nooooo!!!!" she said, sounding shocked, but it only lasted a second. She seemed contemplative for a few minutes and I didn't say a word. "Okay, I can see it. And that really explains so much. He was your first, wasn't he?"

I sighed. "First and only everything really," I confessed.

"What? What about Grayson?" she asked.

I scrunched up my nose at her. I knew how much Ben had always hated him, so when I was twenty and made myself stop sending the letters, I started dating Gray. It was sort of my personal "get-over-Ben campaign," and it didn't work. We'd dated for about six months, if you could even call it dating. Really it was more like hanging out. I couldn't even bring myself to kiss him, though the memories of a vacuum being sucked to my face stalled that one more than Ben's memory. That's basically what it had felt like the first and last time I'd kissed Grayson Ward back in middle school.

He had been more than patient with me, and we'd even had some good times together, but in the end, I'd been dumped for refusing to put out or even make out with him. I'd dated off and on since then, but nothing serious.

"Damn girl, we need to fix this ASAP!"

I didn't know what Peyton had planned, but I was worried I wasn't going to like it.

"I'm not even going to ask," I said, quickly changing the subject. "Does Ruby have Evie today?"

"Yes. I'm only working until one today. Ruby is bringing the girls over and meeting me here, then we're going back to the house to catch up with Maddie. I can't wait to see Eve and Opal with Sara."

"Sara's going to look huge next to those two," I said.

Peyton laughed. "Yeah, you're probably right about that."

Eve wasn't Peyton's biological daughter, but no one would ever suspect that. My sister loved that baby every bit as much as if she were her own flesh and blood. Opal was my sister Ruby's baby. The girls were pretty close to the same age and it was a lot of fun watching them grow up together.

Ruby often watched Eve during the week while Peyton and Oliver worked, though they tried to arrange their schedules to require as little daycare as possible. At first that was for financial reasons, but they were doing more than fine now. They just really loved spending time with Eve.

"I think I'm going to just grab a breakfast sandwich off the counter and head over to Ruby's," I said, ready to jump down from the stool and leave before she could turn the subject back onto me.

"Stop," Peyton said. When I turned to face her, she shoved a plate at me. "Those sandwiches have been sitting out there for nearly an hour. You did not come for that. Go, eat. I just sent food out to Mom and Dad's table, so go join them."

"But I didn't even order yet," I said.

Peyton rolled her eyes and leaned over to kiss my cheek. "Like I didn't know what you wanted."

I looked down at my heaping plate of Peyton's pancakes with sides of bacon, sausage, and ham, because I could never decide between them.

"Thanks, Pey. You're the best!"

I turned and walked back out into the main dining room to rejoin the family.

"I thought you'd left," Mom said. "We would have waited to start eating."

"It's fine," I assured her. "What time are Maddie and Liam getting in?"

"Around lunchtime," Mom practically squealed as she launched into the latest news on Oscar and Sara and everything they'd been up to. Being the one still living at home, I'd already heard it all.

Thirty minutes later I'd finally been able to excuse myself and drove over to Ruby's. She lived in a large apartment over the dairy barn. Ruby loved animals more than any person I knew. I mean, we were shifters, so of course we all had an affinity to the beasts, but Ruby truly loved them. She'd been working out at the ranch since she was just a kid. I'd often been envious of the fact she'd always known what she wanted to do.

Bran and his friend James were working in the dairy when I arrived. I stopped to chat with them for a few minutes before heading upstairs to the apartment.

I didn't bother to knock, just walked in. Ruby was on the floor sitting on a blanket spread out for the girls to play on. They were surrounded by toys but fighting over a plastic cup.

Ruby seemed like the type that would get easily frazzled over something like that, but she'd really chilled out since Opal was born, and loved being a mother. In fact, she'd turned over most of the duties at the dairy to James and only loosely oversaw things now. My sister had always been a workaholic and control freak, so this was a huge change for her.

I joined them on the floor and for one uninterrupted hour I got to just sit back and play with my nieces and talk with my sister about nothing truly important. It was a perfect morning. Then Mom called sounding frantic and I knew I needed to head home and help.

Mom always got super excited but very nervous whenever Madelyn came home, which was rare. I think this was only the third or fourth time since she'd returned to our lives. That meant everything had to be absolutely perfect.

When I walked in, Mom was standing on chair vacuuming the drapes.

"What are you doing?" I asked her.

"I'm cleaning before they arrive. I worry about the dust with Sara being here."

"Mom, you have a housecleaner that does that once a month. She was here yesterday."

"Yes, but I thought I saw a cobweb when I opened the curtains. I just want everything to be perfect."

I sighed and nodded. "Hop down. I'll do it," I said.

"Would you? That would be splendid, Shelby. Thanks. I know I can always count on you." She stepped down with my assistance and gave me a hug as she moved to another room to neurotically check it over.

That was me, the reliable one. There are seven of us kids. I'm number five in the ranking, with Maddie and Thomas following not far behind me. When Maddie disappeared, I'd been a senior in high school. I'd been here for the whole breakdown my mother went through. Poor Thomas took the brunt of it though. She nearly smothered that boy, until our father had to step in and put his foot down.

She hadn't been much better with the rest of us, but everyone scattered off to college or their own homes. I'd stayed. I wasn't even sure anyone realized I was still there. It had been like living in a tomb. Peyton had eventually come back home for a while, but even she had abandoned us during that dark time. I'd had a front row seat for it all.

I'd been the one to hold the fort down, to make certain everyone ate, and Thomas got his schoolwork done. Even when Mom insisted on homeschooling him, she was too depressed to handle most of it, so I did. I'd never resented any of my siblings. I was happy to be there for Mom during that time. She still had her moments, but she was mostly better now. It had changed her in many ways, though. She wasn't the mother we all remembered growing up. I think Maddie sensed that on her last few visits and was making an effort to come home more often.

We were still busy with the final bits of cleaning when Dad pulled up with Maddie and crew. Mom dropped her feather duster and stared at me, frozen.

"Go," I said. "I'll put everything away for you."

"Thank you, Shelby," she said, before practically running towards the front door.

It was great to see Maddie, Liam, Oscar, and Sara. They'd even brought two security guys with them. That always seemed a little weird, but Maddie assured me that was just par for the course of being a Westin. They had been targeted too many times to take any chances, especially with the women and children. The guys didn't hover though, especially in Collier territory, so I didn't even see them until when, by mid-afternoon, Peyton and Ruby still hadn't shown and Maddie asked if she could go with me to check on them.

Liam insisted Jeremiah shadow us since we were leaving Collier territory, even just barely, to go to Peyton's. When we arrived Lizzy, Clara, and Lily were all there, too.

"About time you two showed up," Lily said as she rose to greet Maddie.

"I thought Peyton and Ruby were coming over to Mom's."

"I texted hours ago to tell you to snag Maddie and get your butts over here. It's sister time!" Lily exclaimed, still hugging Madelyn around the neck. "I missed you MC, sooooo much!"

"Oh no, what is she drinking?" I asked.

"Wine," Peyton and Clara said in unison before yelling "Jinx!"

I shrugged and poured two glasses of wine, handing one to Maddie. "Looks like we've got some catching up to do."

Jeremiah had accompanied us but chose to stay out in the front parlor and do his best to ignore us.

As the day turned to evening, Oliver stopped by long enough to deliver pizzas and change clothes.

"Where are you off to tonight, cowboy?" Ruby asked him.

Oliver snorted and shook his head. "I already talked to the guys. Everyone's in agreement that you lushes, I mean luscious ladies, should just stay the night here. I'm taking Brady and Kenneth with me out on the range, so the place is all yours. But who's the creepy guy in my parlor?" Oliver asked.

We all giggled. Brady and Kenneth were Oliver's little brothers. They lived with him and Peyton. There were actually three, but Tim was away at college at the moment.

"That's not creepy, that's Jeremiah," Lizzy corrected him, making very little sense.

"Okay, so who is Jeremiah?" Oliver tried again.

"Maddie's security detail," she said. "I refused one, but then Maddie's an actual Westin and Liam's a paranoid control freak when it comes to his family."

Maddie shrugged and nodded in agreement. "You get used to it. He's part of the Delta team on Westin Force. Patrick's pretty much assigned the poor guy to me."

Patrick O'Connell was head of security for Westin Pack. Let's just say he took security very seriously. I didn't know much about it, but I knew enough to know that Westin Force was basically his own private military. Lizzy's mate, Cole, worked closely with him. She and Cole alternated their time between Westin and Collier Packs. It was still strange to me how drastically my sister had changed after mating him, but there was no doubt in anyone's minds just how happy the two of them were together.

Satisfied with Lizzy's answer, Oliver kissed his mate goodnight, stopped by to talk to Jeremiah for a moment, then headed out leaving just us girls, and Jeremiah, there for the night. It didn't take long at all for Peyton to rat me out.

"Okay, okay, you guys, we have an issue that needs resolving, like yesterday," Peyton said. She had once been the quietest of us all, but mating Oliver had certainly awakened a new assertive side to her.

"What's up?" Lily asked. "This sounds serious."

"Shelby slept with Benjamin Shay!" she blurted out.

I froze, my jaw dropped in shock as all eyes flew to me.

"Wait? Ben's home?" Clara asked.

"When? I just saw his mother two days ago and she didn't mention a thing," Ruby added.

I closed my eyes, praying this was all a nightmare. I didn't want to talk about Ben. I certainly didn't want to talk about sex with Ben. It was all still too painful, and I would not share any of it with them. I didn't care that they were my sisters and overshared everything. This was private, and very personal. I had secrets I had never told anyone, and I didn't plan to start now.

"He's not," I tried to assure them. "I haven't seen or heard from Ben in nearly nine years. This is something that happened a long, long time ago," I said, trying to brush it off and downplay it all.

"Shelbs, I love you, you know that, but you need help, and that's what sisters are for," Peyton said. I wanted to murder her right there. How dare she bring this up! I didn't care how much wine she'd consumed, this was crossing a line she'd never even approached before.

"Is that why you're still pining for him?" Ruby asked.

"What? I'm not," I insisted.

Lizzy and Clara shared a look and burst out laughing.

"Shelby, if anyone knows about wallowing and pining, it's me, hon," Lizzy said. "And you are definitely doing both."

I sighed. So they'd all noticed?

"I very vaguely remember Ben," Lily said. She and Madelyn had met at Alpha camp one summer when they were young and became instant best friends for life, and they still were. Lily had spent plenty of time visiting us while we were growing up, so of course she too knew who we were talking about.

"So all these years you're still hung up on him?" Ruby asked.

"It's really not like that. Peyton's just worried because his brothers are in my seventh grade English class and seeing them all the time has stirred up plenty of old memories, but I'm fine, you guys. I've been over Ben for a long time," I lied, pretty convincingly.

"But you never date," Ruby challenged. She was never one to just let something drop. She was like a dog with a bone when she caught on to something.

"I'm just busy. I'm not opposed to dating. I go out every now and then. I just haven't met the one."

"You can date and have fun while waiting for the one," Ruby reminded me. She certainly had.

"I know that."

"We just need to find her a nice guy to date," Peyton suggested.

"No, that's quite alright," I said.

"Oh, oh, oh, did that hottie come that MC always bring with her?" Lily asked. "Not Jeremiah, the other one," she whispered in a much too loud voice.

"No offense, Jeremiah," Lizzy yelled out.

"None taken," he replied.

"You mean Walker," Madelyn said, then shrugged. "Yeah, I could see it."

"Walker's here?" Lizzy asked.

"Yes. Liam knew I'd want to spend time alone with you guys, so he brought Walker to watch over the kids."

Lizzy nodded. "He is yummy, Shelbs. You could certainly do worse."

"Is he single?" Clara asked.

"Yes," Maddie confirmed. "It's been a few months since he broke up with his last semi-serious girlfriend."

"Great, then it's settled. Shelby will go out on at least two dates with Walker while you guys are in town," Peyton announced.

"This is a terrible idea," I tried to say.

"It's a great idea!" Lily exclaimed.

"Jeremiah, you aren't going to run back and tell him all this, are you?" Lizzy asked.

He never actually came into the room with us, but we all knew with his wolf hearing that he was listening in.

"Unfortunately for Walker, Liam made me sign a full confidentiality agreement for Ms. Maddie. My lips are sealed," he said.

They all giggled. I couldn't help but laugh a little, too.

"Thanks Jeremiah, you're the best!" Maddie hollered back at him.

"Now, let's work out the details," Lily said.

Much to my horror, she pulled over the easel Peyton had set up for Eve to draw on now that she could pull herself to stand, and they started diagraming a plan to get Walker and me together.

"Pass me the bottle," I told Clara. "I'm going to need a lot more wine for this!"

Ben

Chapter 4

"Jake, do it again!" I yelled.

It was his fifth time up a steep incline and back down. Each time I added more weight to his pack. He was currently up to two hundred and fifty pounds and although that cocky smile of his had disappeared two trips ago, the kid was still going.

"Are you trying to kill him?" Jeff asked with a chuckle.

"No," I said. At this point I was too fascinated by him. "Just finding his limit. I'm not sure he has one. This kid just will not stop. What is he? Even for us, this level of strength and endurance is rare." I couldn't hide the admiration in my voice.

"No idea what you're talking about," the major said to me with a wink, reminding me we weren't free to talk openly.

"You really don't know?"

He sighed. "Son, I look for the signs. It's not like there's some magical test I can give to confirm you guys. I just watch and discern, and Jake's been on my radar from day one."

I nodded, not wanting to admit a simple genetics test was all he needed. Fortunately, the military liked to shoot stuff into us, not take blood out, and if they did, it was for basic tests like iron where they weren't looking closely enough to tell the difference. "I can definitely see why, but isn't that a bit risky?"

"How so?"

"What if you're wrong?"

Major Collins threw his head back and laughed. "I'm not. I never am. You're too easy to spot. Can't say I've been able to grab you all. Heck, I'm fighting tooth and nail for Jake right now. Everyone wants him, but my higher ups pulled rank, and the two of you leave tonight. I need to get him out of here before someone else starts really pressing for him."

I nodded, excited to hear I was getting sprung.

"I'll break the news to him when he gets back down," I said.

Jeff smiled. "Give him a break, Shay."

"Maybe," I said.

Collins headed back off to wherever he had come from and I waited.

Jake came down the hill and dropped his pack without a single complaint. He was certainly a determined little shit. I could see the fight still in his eyes. He'd go again without a complaint. He stood at attention and waited for my next order.

"At ease, Jake. Take a break. Hydrate."

He startled and looked a little confused. I hadn't exactly been nice to him for even a second since Collins made me choose him. I resented that I'd been told to pick my guy, and then in the next breath, was strongly advised that it be Jake.

There were two other suspected shifters in the mix, and I wondered what would happen to them. I often thought of what my life in the army would have been like if I hadn't been picked up. Our animal spirits needed to shift on a regular basis. I could do that around my team without consequence. There was no way that would have happened in a regular squadron.

"Take a seat and relax," I told Jake. "Get some water. I'm serious. You've been assigned. We roll out tonight.

He sat down hard and looked humbler than I'd ever seen him before.

"You're serious? I made it?"

I rolled my eyes. "Jake, did you really think there was any chance in hell you wouldn't make it on a spec op team?"

He shrugged. "It's all I've ever wanted to do. You know, be a part of a small forces unit, that brotherhood, and hopefully make a difference in the world, too. I came here determined that I could survive anything thrown my way. That's what got me up the mountain each time. I mean I swear that pack gets heavier every time I put it on."

I threw my head back and laughed. "Open it."

He did without question and his eyes widened. "You've been weighting it?"

"Fifty more pounds each trip up," I admitted.

"But how?" he asked, looking at me.

I grinned. "I have my ways. I'm not so different from you, Jake."

He looked skeptical but didn't comment. Did this kid really think I didn't know who or at least what he was? I tried to see it from his eyes. I was in a damn chair, of course he didn't see me like that. He'd know a shifter would have recovered by now. There were very few things in this world that truly injured our kind.

With Jake's speed I'd originally thought he was some sort of cat, but they didn't often carry the same level of endurance this kid had. I was excited to find out just what kind of shifter he was. I couldn't just come out and ask. As shifters, we were all a little skittish. It took a broken or twisted one to join the military in the first place. I think we all went out for spec ops knowing we were superior in many beneficial ways to humans.

I still remembered when I first got notice of my team. In some ways it's even scarier, because in a team that small and tight, there were no secrets. I knew Jake must be going through all of those emotions now, but I wasn't going to call him out on it.

I'd been taken in by Crawley. He was just a tech guy at the time, and over the last nine years had worked his way up to leader. He was a damn good leader, too. He'd taken me under his wing on day one. Now I know in hindsight that all his talk about, "don't worry, things are going to be okay—you'll find out we're all the same here, no matter what..." and other shit he'd spouted, was supposed to prepare me in some way, for the bomb they were about to drop, once we finally met up with the squad.

We had a very unique introduction for new members. Instead of just letting them know we understood their exceptional situations, and were all shifters too, we blindsided them. No one speaks aloud about that fact, ever. We might talk around it, but the word "shifter" is tacitly forbidden.

So when we blindside a new recruit, we pull him in and make him stand in the middle as we surround him, then we all flash shift on the spot, shredded clothes and everything. It's a shock before the instant relief sets in, and you find out you really aren't alone, and this path you chose really is the right one, and that everything is going to be okay.

Jake was scared, I could tell, and rightly he should be. We all were when we sat in his shoes.

"Everything's going to be okay, Jake. We're all in this together and we understand, your, um, unique situation far better than you think," I said.

His eyes went wide with surprise and questions. I couldn't say anything more than that.

"Go pack. We're flying out to meet with our unit tonight."

"Can I ask what unit?"

I grinned. "We'll talk on the plane."

I was expecting Bulldog to pick us up, but it was a human pilot giving us a lift. As soon as we were in the air, Jake turned to me and started asking questions. I shook my head and shifted my eyes towards the pilot. I hoped he understood I wasn't blowing him off, we just weren't safe to talk freely.

It was only an hour flight before the plane touched down. The guys weren't there to greet us. I already knew they had been given a last second mission and I hated not knowing where they were or if they were okay. Jake seemed to sense my apprehension and kept his mouth shut.

I led the way to our hidden home base. The guys definitely knew I was coming at least, because there were newly laid wooden planks down across any areas they thought my chair may struggle to cross. They were camouflaged with the local terrain as best they could, but I immediately noticed.

Jake kept looking around, taking it all in.

"Are we free to talk here?" he whispered.

I laughed out loud. "Yeah, you're good. The guys are out on mission. Hopefully they'll be back tonight. About damn time they sent me home."

I parked my wheelchair in a corner and stood up to stretch. God, it felt good. I'd only risked it in the shower a few times while stuck on medical.

"Um? You can stand?" Jake said. He looked a little freaked out, like he'd just seen a ghost. How appropriate, I thought.

"Relax, Jake. I'm fine."

"Then why are you using a wheelchair?"

"I was shot, dude. In the spine of all places, that's not something I'm supposed to heal from so quickly."

"But you did," he added.

"Yeah, but I'd turn into an experimental pincushion if they knew that. We all have unique gifts here, Jake. We survive by flying under the radar. I'm sure you can appreciate that."

"Uh, yeah, sure," he said. I sensed he was a little skittish, probably just nervous for his first assignment.

"Damn, it feels good to be home and out of that chair. It's going to take a few days just to stretch the kinks out from being stuck in there."

"What unit is this? I was never told."

I smiled proudly at him. "Have you ever heard of the Ghosts?"

His eyes nearly bugged out of his head. "You're just messing with me," he finally concluded.

"We don't really speak the name aloud, we just simply go by the Ghosts. I'm not shitting with you, Jake. This is one of the most elite teams in the military. We only take the best of the best and look specifically for those with, well, special talents, if you know what I mean."

He looked around in awe. I was certain he still wasn't fully convinced I was telling the truth.

I headed for our small kitchen and fixed a sandwich. The best part about the Ghosts was that we were almost always left alone. We received our assignments on a weekly basis, with the occasional emergency that popped up. Crawley took care of all the paperwork and the rest of us just did our jobs.

When combined forces were necessary, we kept our heads low and worked hard and fast to get in, fulfill our goal, and get back out. We weren't all wolves, but we functioned similar to a small pack, and that gave me plenty of comfort.

Not for the first time, I sniffed the air when Jake walked by, trying to discern what sort of shifter he was. Dude wore this deodorant that was so strong it masked everything else and made my head hurt.

As it was late in the night when we arrived, and there was no sign of the guys, I told Jake to call it a night. I knew he had to be exhausted with everything I'd put him through that day. He didn't argue as he crashed into the bed I directed him to. He didn't even bother changing. He was out the second his head hit the pillow.

I walked through camp checking our supplies and fussing over the mess they'd left behind. I was a little depressed to find they hadn't been home waiting for us to arrive, but I understood, the mission comes first.

I waited up for a few more hours, then certain they weren't coming back anytime soon, I headed for bed and crashed out for the night.

Hours later, I jerked awake when cold water hit my face.

"Good morning, sunshine. Get your ass out of bed, this ain't no fancy hotel where you get to lounge around all day," Crawley said.

"Where's the kid?" Bulldog asked.

I stretched and groaned, then pointed to the top bunk across the room where I'd told Jake to bunk. "Where the hell were you guys last night?"

"Last minute op, just recon, nothing serious," Crawley said.

Bulldog was already descending on Jake with Mike right behind him.

"Don't look like much, does he?" Bulldog asked Mike.

Sam was standing over me. "He's got a pool going already. Want to give me a hint what you think this kid is?"

I snorted. "Count me out. He wears deodorant strong enough to singe my nose hairs."

"Well, Collins says we're stuck with him, so let's get his induction over with already so we can get down to business. It's damn good having you home, Shay," Crawley said.

"Jake, is it?" he asked, approaching the kid who already looked a little freaked out by his sudden wake-up call. "I'm Crawley, leader of this riff-raff. We have a special way we do inductions around here, so up and at'em, let's go."

Jake sighed, but jumped out of bed fully dressed from the night before, boots and all.

"Well he's certainly prepared," Mike commented.

I laughed, knowing in truth he had just been so tired he hadn't even bothered to take them off before crashing.

Crawley walked Jake to the middle of the room and had us all circle up around him. He turned, checking out each person and obviously feeling a bit trapped. That was pretty normal. Our animal spirits didn't exactly like being cornered. It put us all on the defense. Bulldog smiled and nodded at me, clearly remembering that feeling from his own initiation.

"Boys, shift!" Crawley commanded and the six of us all flash shifted into our natural animal forms. We were quite the sight: two bears, a jaguar, a fox, a tiger, and my wolf.

Jake should have felt surprise, then relief at seeing us, but I clearly smelled fear wafting off him. I took a step closer and he backed up, nearly tripping over himself.

"What the hell are you people?" he cried out, his anxiety rising.

Crawley shifted first, as I followed closely behind.

"What the hell is this, Shay?" he demanded.

I looked at Jake, confusion evident in his eyes. He had no idea we were shifters, but worse than that, it was obvious he had no idea shifters even existed.

"Jake, calm down, it's going to be okay," I told him.

Bulldog, who was actually a bear shifter, roared, and the kid nearly leapt into my arms.

"That's just Bulldog, ignore him, and focus. Jake, I need to you look at me and breathe, just breathe."

Mike shifted back. "What are we going to do with him now? I thought you personally tested him," he said to me.

Everyone was suddenly on edge. It couldn't be possible. There was no way Jake could be a human.

"I did, and so did the Major. I'm telling you, he can run circles around all of you. Yeah, even you, Truman," I retorted to the jaguar trying to circle Jake like prey.

At first chance I expected Jake to flee, but when that moment came, he froze and just stood there, staying close to my side.

"What are you?" he finally asked me.

I sighed. "I'm a wolf shifter."

"And-and, you thought I was like you? That I could shift or whatever you call that?" he stuttered.

"Yeah, I did. Major Collins has never been wrong on this before. There are certain signs he's trained to watch for."

"Major Collins is one of you, too?" he asked.

I shook my head. "No, he's human."

"But-but he knows about this?"

I nodded.

"And he goes out of his way to ensure humans don't know about this," Mike said in a threatening tone.

I was impressed that Jake was able to ignore him so easily as he focused solely on me.

"Wh-why me?" he stuttered again.

The kid was white as a ghost and I feared he was going to go into shock.

"Because you're the best of the best, Jake. You outran everyone. I had you packing two hundred and fifty pounds up that mountain yesterday, and you ran with it despite clear exhaustion setting in. That level of endurance, well, quite frankly, it's not human. It's a huge flag that Collins watches for. There were at least two other shifters in contention for this spot and you beat them hands down."

"What happens to them? I mean, are there other units like this?"

"No," I said. "We're the best of the best, period. We all made our choices when we joined. Military life is hard enough without having to hide this part of you all the time. I know you can't possibly understand that, but we're the lucky ones. We don't have to hide here."

"I'm calling Collins. He can deal with this. In the meantime, he's your problem, Shay, until we figure what the hell to do with him," Crawley said.

"Wait, what?" Jake asked, suddenly snapping out of the daze he was in.

"The Verndari have a serum that erases memories. I could probably get my hands on some," Truman offered as he finally shifted back.

"You're kicking me out? Just because I can't change into some kind of animal? That's bullshit! I earned my right to be here, and if Ben’s right and this is the best of the best, the infamous Ghosts, then I’m staying. I’ve worked my ass off to be here. I deserve it,” Jake said

I grinned. “That’s the cocky little shit I’ve been telling you guys about.”

“Jake, it’s our utmost job to keep humans from finding out about us. You’re a liability now. This should never have happened,” Crawley said.

“Well, it did,” Jake said. “So suck it up and deal with it. I can’t hulk out and morph into something I’m not, but I can pull my own weight and be an asset to this team. Okay, so I was surprised. I’m over it now. Who gives a shit what you are? As far as I’m concerned you are my brothers now, and I’m not planning on going anywhere.”

Shelby

Chapter 5

I was nervous and excited for my date with Walker as I got dressed and carefully applied my makeup. We were just having dinner, but he was taking me to a nice place in the next town over that I have been wanting to try.

Maddie and Lizzy had teamed up to introduce us two days ago and I'd only got to talk to him a few times since. He was only here for a week and we were almost halfway into that, but that was one of the things that appealed most to me. There was no chance of commitment. This would just be a strings-free evening out with a man I didn't entirely seem to hate.

There was a knock on the front door at exactly five o'clock. He was certainly punctual. I rummaged through the closet to find the heels I wanted to wear with my little black dress. I rarely had need for them, but didn't mind dressing up, especially for a fancy dinner with a handsome guy, or at least that's what I was trying to convince myself of.

Despite the no-strings-attached clause, I was still a nervous wreck. It had been a while since I'd been on a date. Butterflies swarmed in my stomach as I descended the stairs to find Walker looking dashing in a black suit and talking to my father.

I rolled my eyes, letting the irritation of the scene calm me.

"Shelby, you look lovely tonight," my father said.

"Thanks, Dad, but that's supposed to be his line. I'm not in high school anymore, you don't need to give my date the run down."

Walker laughed. "You really do look beautiful, Shelby."

I blushed a little from his compliment and my nerves turned to actual excitement.

"Fine, I'll leave you two to it, then," my father said, shaking hands with Walker. "Don't forget it's a school night, sweetie," he teased with a wink as he walked away.

I smiled and shook my head. "Sorry about that."

He shrugged. "It's fine. You ready?" he asked, nodding towards the door.

"Yeah, let's do this."

Once in the car I apologized for my dad again. "He really means well," I tried to say, but Walker just brushed it off.

"Honestly, Shelby, it's not a big deal. I've always liked and respected your father."

"So this isn't your first trip to Collier?" I asked, certain we'd never met before.

"No, actually I always accompany Maddie and the kids when they come, and I'm a Longhorn wolf, and I remember him visiting there as a child. He's a good man and he was a great Alpha," he said, instantly warming him to me.

"He is," I said, proudly. "Though since he handed the ropes over to Thomas, I think he's a little lost on what to do with his life. I take the brunt of that, I'm afraid. He's always asking me to go fishing or out for a run with him. I try to oblige as much as possible, but sometimes it would be nice to just live my own life."

"Have you considered moving out and getting your own place then?" he asked. There was no judgement in his voice, just curiosity. It wasn't like it was uncommon for an unmated female to live with her parents until she took a mate.

"Of course I've thought about it, only a million times a day," I laughed.

"So why don't you then?"

I sighed. "It's complicated. I mean, you know Madelyn, of course, so I'm sure you know her history." He nodded. "That was really hard on them. I'd never tell Maddie just how bad it got. She lived through enough without harboring that guilt on top of it. I was the one that stayed to help them through it. Mom basically had a nervous breakdown and battled massive depression for years. Dad and I are pretty close because of it. I guess I feel like they both still need me too much and that it would be selfish of me to move out just for a little solitude."

I didn't know why I was being so open with Walker. He was easy to talk to and made me more comfortable than anyone outside of the family ever had . . . well, except for Ben.

I looked Walker over with his dark hair and bright blues eyes. He was very easy on the eyes and I suspected he could have any woman he wanted. He was panty-melting hot with the air of confidence that oozed sex appeal.

My lady parts clenched at the thought. It was the first physical response I'd had to a man since I was eighteen, and I had to admit, a part of me was relieved by it. I had often wondered if I had been broken beyond repair in that department with everything that had happened.

Sadness threatened to creep in at the thought, but I pushed it away. Those memories would not haunt me tonight. I was determined not to let them. Peyton thought it was all about Ben, but she was wrong. There was so much more to it.

"I think it's very admirable and shows your true character that you care so much about them," Walker said, breaking me from my memories.

I smiled. "Thanks."

We chatted about lighter things for the remainder of the drive.

The steakhouse he took me to was a nice, upscale one. We didn't have too many of those in this area. He pulled up to the front and let the valet park the car. There was something about Walker that was so commanding. I felt strong, important, and maybe even a little sexy on his arm.

He had called ahead and made reservations for us, so we were seated immediately. Conversation continued to flow seamlessly between us with no awkward moments. The longer I was with Walker the more relaxed I became until I realized I was actually enjoying myself on a real date with a very handsome man.

"So, what's it like being stuck watching Oscar and Sara on trips like this?" I asked.

Walker grinned flashing an irresistible matching set of dimples. "They're really good kids. Easiest gig I have going on. I almost wish they'd travel more often. I love kids and hope to have several myself someday."

Sadness threatened to consume me, but I pushed it aside and nodded. "Me too," I managed. "But for now, I'm happy spoiling my nieces and nephew knowing I can hand them back at any time."

We both laughed and he raised his glass in agreement to that. Drinks were flowing freely as we devoured appetizers, salads, and soup before the main course arrived. Normally I was a bit self-conscious about eating on a date, but not this time. I barely even noticed as he ordered for us and food, drinks, and conversation continued throughout the evening.

I was sad to see it come to an end with a triple chocolate cake that was to die for.

After dinner, as we waited for the valet, I told him, "Thanks for tonight. I had a wonderful time. I'm sorry to see it end."

"Unfortunately Sara's an early riser, and if I understood your father correctly, you have school tomorrow. What are you studying? I think that may be the only thing we didn't cover already tonight."

I giggled feeling a little tipsy from all the wine I had drank. "Not studying, I'm a teacher. I teach middle school English."

"I'm impressed. That's very admirable, and somehow quite fitting, I think."

"Well, thanks. It's a recent career after trying out various jobs around Collier. This is my first year teaching full-time."

"How's it going?"

"So far, so good. I love it really. I love the kids and how busy but rewarding it is."

We continued to chat about my job, and he opened up a little more about his on the drive home. All too soon we sitting in his car in front of my house.

He walked me to the door. When I turned to say goodbye, Walker kissed me. At first I froze up, and then things felt a little awkward, but he was patient and kind with me, as he had been all evening. I relaxed and kissed him back. It was nice. Not an all-consuming passionate kiss, but certainly not a vacuum-cleaner-to-the-face sort of kiss, either.

He was a gentleman and said goodbye at the door without pressing things further. We agreed to see each other again the next day. When I said goodnight and made myself walk in the house, I turned to give him one final wave before shutting the door. I leaned back against it and smiled. I had genuinely had a good time with Walker, and it felt like this huge weight had been lifted from my shoulders.

It was late and I didn't think anyone was still awake as I quietly walked upstairs to my bedroom. The first thing I noticed as I started to change into bed clothes was the picture of me and Ben from our senior prom stuck into the side of the mirror. I lovingly traced it with my finger, not allowing the pain it usually brought to consume me.

With a grin, I climbed into bed and turned on the lamp on the nightstand. I reached into the drawer and pulled out stationery and a pen. It had become a bedtime tradition, but after tonight, I was ready to move on.

Dear Ben,

This will be the last time I write to you. I think I'm finally ready to say goodbye and let the past stay in the past. I met someone tonight. His name is Walker. I think you'd like him. No, he's not "the one" and I doubt anything will come of it, but he opened my eyes and my heart to the possibility of love again. In order for that to happen, I have to let you go. You don't have to worry about me anymore. I'm going to be okay.

All my love,

Shelby

I stared at the letter I'd just written, letting the emotions seep in. I nodded, knowing it was the right thing to do. I placed it in an envelope and sealed it, added a little heart sticker to the back, and then wrote the date on the front. I got up and added it to the box on the top shelf of my closet, then put my stationery away and turned out the light.

Ben

Chapter 6

True to his word, Jake stuck it out. He had come to me later that day and asked for advice. I told him to keep his head down, his mouth shut, and do whatever they said. Much to my shock, the kid actually listened.

He was my responsibility and I was supposed to be training him in my job. Turned out he was a really good shot. It took a couple tries and tweaks to compensate for wind trajectory with the sniper rifle, but he was a quick study and soon was out-shooting our backup shooter and impressing everyone.

The others wanted him out. They wanted to hate him. It only took one emergency call for Jake to earn his spot, and much to everyone's surprise, it wasn't as a shooter.

We'd been called in for another recon assignment. This time we were given two tickets to the opera where we needed to get in and plant bugs in two of the boxes. The guys thought it would be fun to watch Jake crash and burn. Crawley gave me the two tickets at the last minute and advised me and Jake to go in.

I tried to argue with him. This wasn't my area of expertise by any means, but they thought the chair might give me sympathy and be an easy distraction so Jake could sneak in and place the bugs.

That's exactly how the first box went down. I "accidently" got too close to the top of the stairs and as several people ran to assist me, it left the opening we needed. Jake was in and out almost as fast as Truman or Mike would have been.

But the interest in me had already died down by the time he reached the second box. Security stopped him, and I couldn't exactly cause another big scene without raising suspicions. I tried to signal to Jake to abort, but he wasn't listening. Instead, he struck up a conversation with the guard.

I couldn't hear a word they were saying over all the chatter, but it took no time at all for him to disappear behind the curtain. He came out a few minutes later, still talking away. He shook hands with the guy and said goodbye as he casually walked back out and down the stairs, giving an imperceptible nod to me as he passed.

I moved to the elevators and followed him back down. We exited the building at different times, and Mike picked us up around the corner.

Truman was laughing his ass, off having heard everything through the wire. He went on and on about how Jake had schmoozed it up with the guy. It became the ongoing joke that Jake could talk his way out of a brown paper bag, and much to Crawley's displeasure, Jake had quickly weaseled his way onto the team.

A week before Thanksgiving, Jake was still with us. Crawley was still bitching about it too, but the rest of the guys had accepted our human brother into the pack. He became a useful negotiator and all-around con man, which was something we never realized we were missing in our unit.

That fateful day, we were called in to assist one of the Ranger units that had come under heavy fire. Our mission was just to get them out safely. It wasn't an uncommon order for us. We were always saving humans' asses; it was just part of the job.

I abandoned my chair to join, providing eyes from above. The guys on the ground were in and out quickly, with only one more soldier remaining.

Crawley went in for the last one. He was clearly injured as I watched from my scope. I scanned the area and a flash of light caught my eye. I zeroed in on it and found the enemy quickly.

"Papa Bear, you've got company to the west, about twenty yards and closing in. Staying hidden so far, so keep your head down. If he comes out, I'll take him," I said through our private radio.

Suddenly, the guy opened fire.

"Shit! I don't have a shot," I yelled. "Get the hell out of there."

Crawley was in the open, exposed. I wanted to throw up when I saw him drop the soldier he was carrying to cover him.

I fired a shot hoping to distract the shooter, but it only stalled him temporarily. He was on the move, and fast now. I could see flashes between breaks in the wall as he ran towards them. I estimated his timing and fired accordingly, but I only managed to nick the bastard.

Mike ran to intersect with his gun at the ready. Bulldog and Truman circled in from behind. Suddenly another shot rang out and I watched as Jake leapt in front of Crawley and covered them both with his body. He took a hit.

"Sniper!" I yelled, as I quickly identified his position and easily gave a kill shot. "Sniper has been terminated."

"All clear down here," Mike called out after taking down the lone gun on the ground.

"Jake's been hit," Crawley said. "Need a medic."

"I'm fine," Jake retorted as he stood and helped Crawley up, then assisted in carrying the wounded soldier to safety.

The mission had been sloppy, but we came out almost unscathed. Once back at camp we learned that Jake really had been shot, right in the buttcheck. It was a graze really, but after that, Crawley gave Jake the nickname of Sugar Cheeks and finally welcomed him to the family.

When a man willingly takes a gunshot for you, doesn't much matter if he's shifter or human, at that point he's just a brother.

As we celebrated that night, the main phone rang. It was only used for absolute emergencies. Everyone fell quiet as Crawley answered.

"Crawley here," he said. "Yeah. Shit. Okay. You have his flights already arranged? Well why the hell not? Have it ready by the time he gets to the airport or all hell is going to break lose. I will. Thanks."

He hung up and turned back to us.

"Ben," he said, and I shook my head. Whatever it was it wasn't good, and I didn't want to hear it. "I'm sorry, man. It's your dad."

"What? My dad? What happened?" I managed to say. I was already turning emotionally numb. It was my default setting in any crisis, and I was bracing for the worst.

"Apparently there was an accident out on the ranch. Your dad's been hurt pretty badly. Bad enough that the major has approved immediate family leave for you. He'll have your flights booked and ready by the time we get you to the civilian airport."

I vaguely remember packing my stuff and saying goodbye. The whole team insisted on riding to the airport to see me off. I knew if they could, they'd all be flying home with me. I had no real information on what had happened or even if he was still alive. My parents were true mates and fully bonded, so if he died, so would my mother. No one had mentioned her so far, and I held on to the hope that meant they were both still alive.

It took almost thirty-six hours to get back to Wyoming. I was exhausted and jet lagged when my plane landed. Thomas Collier met me personally. I had always known him as Shelby's little brother. Of course I knew he would someday be Alpha, and I'd heard the moment he had assumed the position, but it was just hard not to see him as the little kid I knew when I left town. He wasn't that kid anymore, though, he was a full-grown man with a commanding presence.

"Ben, welcome home," he said. "I wish it were under better circumstances."

"Thomas," I said, shaking his hand. "It's good to see you. Now what the hell is going on? I haven't received any information aside from it was urgent that I come home immediately."

"I'm sorry, Ben. Your dad was in an accident at the ranch. Someone lost control of one of the tractors. Your dad's leg is shattered. We were able to medevac him to a facility. They were able to save his leg, but since the bone was so fragmented it required extensive rods to stabilize it."

"He'll never shift again," I whispered. I had seen it once before and heard the stories of shifters who had taken gunshots with similar damage. We healed fast, but if the bone was too shattered there was no repairing it. The artificial rods and screws would keep him from shifting. It was a fate worse than death for our kind.

"I'm so sorry. He'll walk again in time, but he'll never shift again. He and your mom discussed it. He said he'd rather walk in his skin and never shift than to amputate the leg and struggle in skin and fur for the rest of his life."

I nodded, still emotionally numb as I tried to absorb what he was telling me.

"Is Mom with him?"

Ben shook his head. "She was with him through the surgery last week, but then came back home to be with your brothers. They're struggling. She asked me not to call you home, but I overruled her."

"Damn right you should have, too," I murmured. I hated the thought of her going through this alone and worrying about bothering me over it. I tried to curb the anger that flared at the thought. I knew I hadn't really been there for them since I joined the army, but damn it, this was important, and family came first.

I stared out of the window in silence as we drove. As we entered Collier territory, I cracked the window and welcomed the familiar smells. The sights, the memories, it was all so overwhelming. I'd called a lot of places home over the years. Usually it was where my unit was, but that didn't pack quite the same punch as Collier, Wyoming.

Thomas drove me straight home. From the outside it looked like something from a time capsule. Nothing had changed in the last nine years. I took the front steps two at a time and walked in without knocking.

Mom was sitting in the living room, and startled. I think she had dozed off waiting there.

"Ben?" she asked in a sleepy voice.

"Hi, Mom," I said.

"It's really you?"

I smiled and nodded as she rose. I hesitated only a second before swooping her up in my arms. She was small and frail to me now. I could see how she'd aged in my absence, and she looked weak and tired.

"I'm here, Mom. Everything's going to be okay."

Thomas said a quick hello but left us to catch up. She filled me in on more details about Dad and told me all about my twin brothers. They were now twelve and in the seventh grade.

"Where are they?" I asked. I wanted to see for myself that Troy and Will were really okay.

"They're at school. Your daddy and I decided it would be best to get them back to a normal schedule. Today's their last day before Thanksgiving break." She started to tear up as she said it.

"What is it?"

She reached for my hand and held on, almost like she was scared I was going to disappear before her eyes. "You're here and I'll have you home for Thanksgiving. All my babies under one roof for the first time in almost a decade."

Guilt set in as I thought about it.

"Shelby will be happy to see you, too," she surprised me by saying.

I had purposefully avoided thinking about her, pushing it aside every time I so much as thought her name, but being back in Collier it was nearly impossible not to remember. Everything reminded me of her because there wasn't an inch of this place that I didn't have a story that started with "Shelby and I . . ."

I had no plans to see Shelby. Even after all this time, I wasn't sure my heart could handle it, but I didn't want to upset Mom further by saying so.

"I think the boys are in their last class of the day. Why don't we head over to the school and surprise them," she said.

"Sure, let me just change first."

"No, please. You look so handsome in your uniform. Let me show you off."

I smiled and nodded. I would do anything for her, even though I was pretty certain I smelled after two days straight of traveling and no shower. I didn't mention that though. I was tired to my bones, but I could hold off sleep a little while longer to put a smile on my brothers' faces.

Mom insisted on driving us herself and holding on to my arm as I escorted her into the school. It was so surreal and hard not to think back to my first day of seventh grade walking into the building. Too many memories lurked around every corner.

I plastered a grin on my face and mentally reminded myself it was all for Mom.

We stopped first at the office as she proudly introduced me around as if I hadn't grown up knowing pretty much everyone there. They had either been working the same job when I went to school there, or the younger ones were all people I'd attended with. In a town like Collier, everyone knew everyone. Still, I smiled and greeted each of them.

"The boys are both in English right now, just down the hall, third door on the left," the receptionist told us. "You can just go on down and surprise them."

"Thank you," I said.

Once in the hallway I asked Mom, "Do the twins even know I'm here?"

She shook her head. "No. It's been hard enough on them. I didn't want to get their hopes up until I knew for certain you were here. I know how plans can change in a hot minute in the military."

Guilt punched me in the gut knowing the truth was that each vacation home that I had planned, I'd chickened out and went somewhere else while blaming it on the army. I wouldn't even be here now if I had been given any other choice.

Mom knocked and opened the door. "Hi, sorry to interrupt, but we're springing Troy and Will a little early today." She giggled as she pulled me into the room.

I barely recognized the boys as they jumped up and ran towards me, both throwing their arms around me.

"Ben!" Will yelled.

"You're actually home!" Troy exclaimed.

Much to my surprise, I had to calm my wolf. He was getting very agitated and the hair on the back of my neck was standing up. I had heard about post-traumatic stress syndrome and the symptoms, but I'd never expected to experience them myself, especially in a room full of pre-teens.

Then I smelled it, or rather, her. The familiarity of her scent nearly bowled me over. My eyes darted around the room, landing on the teacher up front. I had to blink a few times before reality registered. Shelby.

Mine, my wolf growled in my head. *What the hell?*

Shelby

Chapter 7

I stood there in shock, my pulse racing, my jaw probably touching the floor, as I fought a dizzy spell taking over. Ben Shay was standing in my classroom. My eyes saw him, but my heart was in disbelief. I rubbed my eyes a few times and tried to slow my breathing. I was on the verge of passing out from hyperventilating.

Our eyes locked and my skin began to crawl. *Mine,* my wolf said clearly in my head.

"Ms. Shelby, are you okay?" Caroline asked, jolting me back to reality.

I was standing in front of my class. I could not—no, I would not faint in front of them. I managed a convincing smile even though it felt foreign on my lips. "I'm fine, sweetie. Troy, Will, have a great Thanksgiving break. In lieu of your brother coming home, you do not have to write the essay scheduled over break. Enjoy your family time," I said, impressed with how steady my voice sounded.

"Yes! You're the best," Troy said, running over to hug me before returning to Ben, who I was trying desperately to ignore.

John raised his hand.

"Yes, John?"

"But Ms. Shelby, that's not fair."

"Relax, I'm cancelling the essay for everyone."

That brought cheers from the rest of my class seconds before the final bell rang.

"Happy Thanksgiving. Enjoy your break," I told them as they all got up and scrambled to leave.

Ben was still standing in my doorway, staring at me like he'd just seen a ghost. The activity and excitement of the holiday had the kids pushing him through the door and into the hallway.

"Caroline, shut the door behind you on your way out, please," I said.

She smiled. "Sure, Ms. Shelby. See you next week."

"Bye, sweetie," I said.

The second the door was closed, I sat down hard in my desk chair and had to put my head between my knees for a few minutes to calm myself.

When I felt like I could handle it, I grabbed my phone and dialed Peyton's number. She picked up on the first ring.

"Aren't you in school? Why are you calling me?" she asked.

"Technically school just let out, and technically I'm freaking out!"

"Calm down, Shelbs, Just breathe, you sound like you're on the verge of hyperventilating."

"That's because I am."

"What's wrong? What happened?" she asked, suddenly upset and feeding off my emotions.

"Ben's here," I spat out.

"Your Ben?" she asked.

"Yes, my Ben," I said. *Mine,* my wolf agreed.

"When? Where?"

"I don't know, Pey. He just waltzed right into my classroom today to pick up the twins. He was in uniform and he looked so good. I didn't want him to look that good. I just really started to move on with my life, but it's worse than that."

"Shelby, it can't be that bad," she said, trying to calm me down.

"It is, because my wolf still wants to claim him."

"What does that even mean?"

"I don't know. You tell me!"

"You said he wasn't your one true mate," she reminded me.

"I know what I said, Peyton. I haven't seen him since we were eighteen years old. We weren't mated when he left, but my wolf has always been protective of him since the moment she surfaced, but then I've always been protective of him, so I just figured that was me. But it's not going away. Why isn't it?"

"I don't know sweetie, unless . . ."

"Do not say what I think you're going to say!"

I hung up the phone. I didn't want her to say aloud the words I was thinking, fearful they would somehow make them truer. I had finally begun to put that part of me to rest. I hadn't written him in almost two months, since the night of my first date with Walker.

Walker and I still talked every day. We had agreed weeks ago we were better off just as friends, but I felt like I'd be lying not to tell him. He had helped me deal with a lot of things in his own crazy way and I'd opened up about Ben to him more than I'd ever done with anyone, even Peyton. I still didn't tell him everything, and he suspected as much, but I told him a lot.

With my phone still in my hand. I sent him a quick text.

ME: Ben just showed up out of the blue.

WALKER: Your Ben?

ME: Yes, my Ben. Why is that the first thing everyone keeps asking?

WALKER: Because we thought he was halfway around the world.

ME: Apparently not.

WALKER: Makes sense after his Dad and all.

ME: Guess so.

WALKER: You okay?

ME: No. Yes. I don't know.

WALKER: Working, can I call tonight?

ME: Yeah, thanks. Ttyl

After finishing the conversation with him, I sat there at my desk for a few more minutes. When I figured the coast was clear, I packed up a few things, and snuck out the back door. I needed time to process the fact that Ben was home.

Of course a part of me was thrilled. He changed, but he looked great, and that pissed me off. I quickly checked my appearance the second I got in the car. Decent, I confirmed. At least I had that going for me.

On the drive home I was a little hazy, lost in old memories that were threatening me. Mom was waiting when I arrived.

"Did you see Ben yet?" she asked. She looked excited and I didn't want to disappoint her with my personal freak out.

"Yeah, he came by my classroom to pick up the boys a little while ago."

"Marnie is so excited to have him home, and relieved. He can focus on the boys and she won't feel so guilty now leaving them during Don's recovery. She had confided in me a few days ago the possibility and called this morning to tell me he was on the way. She hadn't wanted to tell anyone, especially the twins, until she knew it was certain. I don't think he's been home since he left to join the army," Mom rambled on.

"No, he hasn't," I said.

"I know how close the two of you used to be. So I gave him a few days to settle in, but Wednesday night he's coming over for dinner. It'll give you two a chance to catch up." She smiled happily and patted my arm before heading into the kitchen.

I tried to fight down the panic and ran to my room.

Was I happy he was back? I asked myself. No. Yes. Maybe. I still couldn't answer that honestly even to myself.

I didn't know how to be around him with all these crazy feelings bubbling out of me. Plus, I felt such guilt over everything, that I wasn't sure I could even look him in the eye. Nine years. Where the hell had he been that was so important for the last nine years? I let loose the anger that surfaced every time I let myself think about that.

He'd missed so much. He hadn't stayed in contact and worse, he hadn't even asked how I was. Nothing. He returned out of the blue and just stood there without saying a word to me. It didn't matter how possessive my stupid wolf felt towards him, she'd always had a soft spot for Ben. I couldn't let that cloud my judgement.

I didn't know how long he would stick around this time, but Mom said he'd been called home, so that meant he'd be heading back. He was going to leave me again and I wouldn't see or even hear from him for probably another nine years.

Nope, I wasn't going to fall for that. My best course of action was to smile prettily and pretend I was perfectly fine, and steer as far the hell away from Ben Shay as physically possible.

Why the school made us have classes on Monday if they were giving off Tuesday through Friday this year made zero sense. Tuesday was officially marked as a teacher workday. I hadn't planned on going in, but if I was to stay low while he was in town, I might as well do something productive where no one would expect to find me.

I allowed myself to wallow for the remainder of the evening, then fell asleep to fresh tears. I hadn't let myself cry for so long that it was almost therapeutic. When Walker called I didn't even bother to answer it.

The next morning, I got up and headed into work early, grabbing a bagel from the kitchen on my way out instead of stopping at Kate's for breakfast.

I knew Walker would worry that I hadn't talked to him. He worried about a lot of things and seemed to carry the weight of the world on his shoulders. So, I shot off a quick text when I got to my classroom.

ME: Sorry I missed your call. Pity party and early bed.

ME: I'm fine!

WALKER: I'm on parameter detail today. Call anytime if you need to talk.

ME: Thanks. Working today too.

WALKER: Thought you were taking it off.

ME: I know. Hiding. Just call me a coward.

WALKER: You're going to have to face him sooner or later.

ME: Why? He's just going to leave again.

WALKER: But what if he doesn't come back next time. Now's your chance for real closure.

ME: I've found my closure, or close enough.

WALKER: Liar.

I stared down at the screen with a frown. I hated when he spoke the truth.

For the next several hours I attempted to bury myself in work. All outstanding papers were carefully graded. We only had three weeks of school left after Thanksgiving and I had all of it prepped and ready before lunch, which I skipped.

The afternoon was spent cleaning like a madwoman. No one even stopped by to check on me or even say hi, because they all knew I was blowing off the day, as were most of the teachers at the school.

I swore I could see my own reflection in the floor by the time I was done scrubbing. Physical labor and cleaning had always been helpful to my sanity. My family knew when I got like this to just stay away because I was working through something. Usually by the time I was done after a mad cleaning binge, I felt a million times better, and whatever was bothering me, was laid to rest.

But that nagging, itching feeling that had started the second Ben Shay walked in my classroom was not letting up. I knew I needed to go for a run.

Not chancing crossing paths with him, I packed up and headed to Peyton's. No one was home when I got there, and for that I was grateful. I stripped on her back porch and ran. The area stunk a bit like Larken territory with a hint of Collier. Their scent wasn't that different from our own, so I pushed past it and ran until nightfall.

I'd been out there for hours and still my wolf and I could not find peace. All she wanted to do was turn tail and run back to Collier . . . back to Ben. She was in mourning for him all over again.

He's not our mate. He's just our friend, or he was once upon a time. Now he's nothing to us. I tried to reason with her, or maybe I was just trying to reason with myself.

Spending time in my fur should have made me feel better, but I felt worse when it was all said and done. Peyton was sitting on the back porch waiting for me when I finally returned to my skin.

She handed me my clothes without saying a word about it.

"Saved you some dinner. I'm about to put Eve down if you want to say hi."

I nodded, dressed quickly, and followed her into the house.

"Thanks. Skipped lunch so I'm starving," I confessed.

She frowned at me, but I turned my attention to Eve when she toddled in with Kenneth following carefully behind her.

"She's getting too good at that," I commented on Eve's recently acquired walking skills. She was even beginning to run a little as she giggled at Kenneth like he was chasing her.

"Too good," Peyton confessed. "I have some good news, though."

"You're pregnant?" I asked.

She laughed. "Not yet, but hopefully soon. I've officially gone off birth control. Eve will be turning one soon and we don't want to wait to add to our crazy little family."

I hugged her and wished her well. There was nothing little about Peyton's family. When she'd taken Oliver as a mate, she did so knowing he was a package deal with not just Eve, but three nearly grown brothers he had raised since they were toddlers, and he was only like eleven or something at the time. I couldn't even imagine it. She called them her boys and had a protective nature that rivaled the strongest Pack Mother.

They lived between packs, as did Lizzy and Cole. That meant they pledged allegiance to both packs. I didn't understand how it was possible, but they made it work. In Lizzy's case it seemed easier because we were strong allies with Westin Pack, but the Larken wolves had been our enemies for nearly as long as I could remember.

Peyton and Oliver were working closely with their respective Alphas to help try and mend the packs history. There was even talk of a possible merger of the two packs.

I rinsed my plate and put it in the dishwasher when I was done, then helped tuck Eve in for the night before saying goodbye. I could tell Peyton wanted to talk and make certain I was really okay, but I didn't wait around for that.

As I drove through town on my way home, I somehow knew without a doubt in my mind that Ben was at the bar as I passed it. It was like I could feel his presence there and it sort of freaked me out. I'd always had an awareness towards him, but this was at a whole new creepy level.

Ben

Chapter 8

I sat at the bar letting reality finally sink in. I'd made a huge mistake. Shelby wasn't mated to that weasel Grayson. It had all been a lie. Maybe she liked him at the time, maybe she didn't. I couldn't trust anything I thought anymore.

I knew she had been acting strangely, but I feared I may have jumped the gun on why. Seeing her standing there looking at me like I was a damn ghost had shaken me to my core. She wasn't the girl I once knew. She was now this gorgeous woman who took my breath away.

The worst part was that my wolf was adamantly trying to claim her. I was struggling to believe it myself, but Shelby Collier might very well be my one true mate. I spent a late night at the bar pondering that thought.

Then first thing this morning, I'd tried to find her. It was easy to get the information I needed from Mom. Shelby was still single. She lived at the Alpha house with her parents and taught English at the middle school. Her mother seemed happy to see me when I stopped by, but Shelby wasn't home, and no one seemed to know where the hell she was.

It was a teacher's workday, but she'd made other plans for the day, though no one seemed to know exactly what those plans were.

“She said she’d be home for Thanksgiving, so I doubt she went to see Walker,” Cora had said.

“Who’s Walker?” I asked, and it still felt like I’d been throat punched just remembering her answer as I tried to calm my wolf and fought to control my breathing. My hands fisted tightly of their own accord.

“Oh, Walker’s her boyfriend dear, but it’s a long-distance thing. Great guy. We all love him.”

I was going to have to put a stop to that right away. Shelby was mine. She had always been mine, I was just too stupid and jealous to realize it.

I wracked my brain trying to remember everything leading up to the day I lost it and joined the army. I didn’t exactly regret the decision, but now would I do it again, knowing the truth that I’d mistakenly stepped aside for a lying asshole when I could have been here to protect my girl?

I had read every letter Shelby had ever sent me and I went on a weeklong drinking binge that I do not remember at all when her letters stopped arriving. I still kept them all and read them frequently. When times were tough, they were what pushed me through.

I had wanted to write her back, but my pride wouldn’t allow it. She’d never once written a word about Grayson to me, that had always pissed me off, but now I understood that was because there had never been anything between them to write about, and I was the fool.

I shot back another two fingers of whiskey, hoping the fire would calm me. It did not.

For a moment I swore I felt her presence nearby, and I slapped some twenties on the counter and walked outside. Her scent was fresh in the air, but faint at the same time. I knew she had driven past the bar in the last few minutes. I shouldn’t be that aware of her, unless it was true, and Shelby really was my true mate.

Another punch of guilt hit me. She had poured her heart out to me after her sister had disappeared. I should have been here comforting her through that pain. I’d missed so much in the last nine years, only further evidenced by my not-so-little brothers.

Troy was holding back from me, distant, like he was afraid to get too close, but Will was wide open and stayed glued to my side like he was terrified that I'd vanish into thin air if he let me out of his sight.

I had never once allowed myself to consider how my decisions had impacted my family and those I'd left behind. They say that giving your life to serve your country was the ultimate sacrifice, but being back here, now, it felt like the ultimate betrayal to everyone I loved. I was struggling to deal with that revelation.

Would it have been better if I had stayed? What kind of man would I be today?

Would it have been better if I had kept in contact more? Called more? Sent responses to the letters Shelby wrote me?

I had made my commitment and adding guilt on top of it would only have caused potential distraction and harm to my unit. I had to believe I'd done the right thing.

One of the letters Shelby had written to me had always haunted me the most. She had sent a series of them while I was away at boot camp telling me she had some exciting news she couldn't wait to share.

I had called her and asked her not to come, to allow me time with my family. It was the last time I had heard her voice before yesterday. She had cried and begged me to let her come, but in the end, she'd accepted my request and hadn't shown.

A few weeks later as I was settling into the unit, she wrote that none of it mattered anymore. She sounded depressed and I swore the spots on the paper were tears. Something in my gut had told me to call and check on her, but I hadn't. To survive out there, I needed to cut ties to Shelby, so I had. I couldn't look back and regret that decision now, no matter what.

Cora Collier had invited me to dinner the next day, and at the rate things were going, it was my best chance to finally see Shelby and start getting the answers I so desperately needed to all these questions.

First thing the next morning, I took the boys fishing. The second we arrived, I knew it was a bad idea. Everywhere I looked I saw flashes of memories of Shelby. She was everywhere because she had been my everything.

I didn't let the memories make me sad, though. They were great and I held on to the happiness I once felt with the hope we'd get back to that place again. I didn't know if it was possible, but I was damn sure going to try.

"Ben, I got something," Will yelled.

I walked over just in time to help him pull in a large trout.

"Looks like we have lunch for today, boys," I said with a hoot.

Will beamed, but Troy was still being a bit standoffish to me.

"Troy, look at this thing," I said, trying to encourage him to join in.

"It's a fish. What a shocker," he said sarcastically.

I didn't know how to get through to him, but I was determined to keep trying.

I made a small fire right next to the stream and cleaned and cooked the trout. We had packed a lunch just in case we didn't catch anything. I took the downtime to talk to the boys. As suspected, Will talked like he had diarrhea of the tongue, while Troy answered in clipped, direct short answers.

By the time we were back home, nothing had really changed, and I hadn't made any real progress with Troy, but I hoped that just having memories with me would help in the long run. I grabbed a quick shower and dressed for the evening.

"Where are you going?" Will asked when I came downstairs ready to leave.

"I'm having dinner at the Alpha house," I said.

"Really? Cool!" Will said. "We've never had dinner there before. Will Thomas be there?"

I shrugged. "I'm not sure."

He crinkled up his nose like maybe my evening wasn't as impressive as he imagined it to be.

"So you're having dinner with his parents?" he tried to clarify.

"Yes."

"Will Ms. Shelby be there?" Troy asked.

"Yes, or at least I hope she will."

"You were an asshole to leave her the way you did. She was supposedly your best friend. She's a really good person, and you're just going to hurt her again. It would be best if you just stayed away," Troy said, staring me down.

I was taken aback by the venom in his voice. Was that really how he felt? Did everyone feel that way?

"Troy," I started, but he just stood up, shook his head, and dismissed me as he headed for his room and slammed the door shut. I looked over at Will. "Do you feel that way too?" I asked out of curiosity.

He shrugged. "We were pretty little when you left. I don't remember it all that much. Ms. Shelby has told us a few stories about you growing up. She says Caroline and I remind her a lot of you guys. Was Ms. Shelby really your best friend when you were my age?"

"Yeah, she was. She's been my best friend my entire life."

Will frowned and shook his head. "Maybe she was, but I'm pretty sure you blew that badly."

"What do you mean?"

He shrugged again. I was beginning to hate that shrug. It seemed like it was his go-to answer to everything. I stared him down until he caved.

"It's just, whenever we mention you, she gets sad. It makes Troy mad. It makes me extra cautious not to hurt Caroline. I don't ever want to see that look on her face."

"What look?" I asked before I could stop myself.

"Like you died and took a piece of her with you."

His words gutted me. Was that really how Shelby felt? More than ever I needed to get over there and see her now. Will left the room while I was deep in thought, trying to figure out exactly what to say to her. I had considered myself a confident guy, but I was terrified to face Shelby knowing how badly I'd screwed things up. I didn't have a clue how to even start trying to fix it.

Hey Shelby, it's been a while.

Shelby, it's Ben. Funny story . . .

I may have made a big mistake.

Sport, I'm still crazy in love with you, please give me a second chance.

The whole drive over I thought through my best possible opening lines, but none of them felt right.

I was half an hour early when I parked and walked up to the front door. My palms were sweating, and I felt like I might throw up, but I was also really excited to see my girl. As I raised my hand to knock, the door flew open and Shelby rushed out, plowing right into me.

Instinctively my arms wrapped around her waist and I pulled her to me to steady her. My heartbeat raced with the familiarity of holding her.

"Hi," I managed to say as I looked down into eyes that were wide with shock.

Shelby

Chapter 9

I couldn't breathe. His scent enveloped me, making my head spin as the realization began to sink in. Ben was holding me. My wolf hummed with happiness and I hadn't felt so content since, well, since the last time I'd been in his arms.

As the fog started to clear in my head, I pushed back against his solid chest.

"Let me go," I demanded. "What are you even doing here? You're early. You're never early," I said.

I was upset. It might have been a chicken shit move, but at the last minute I'd decided I wasn't ready to face Ben, so I was leaving before he got there. Why was he here now?

"Sorry. Army habit," he said in a voice deeper than I remembered. It buzzed through my body like I'd been struck by a livewire.

"Well, stop it," I said, before righting myself and pushing past him.

"Where are you going?" he asked.

I sighed. "Out."

"But we're having dinner in twenty minutes." He looked down at his watch to confirm the time.

"No, you're having dinner with my parents in twenty minutes," I informed him. The looks of disappointment and frustration on his face amused me.

“Come on, Sport. Why are you running? Stay for dinner. It’s been too long,” he said.

My traitorous heart nearly melted. I had to find a way to protect it before Ben destroyed me forever. I wasn’t sure I was strong enough to survive another broken heart.

“You don’t get to call me that anymore,” I said defiantly, even while everything inside me screamed to run back into his arms. Instead, I crossed them over my chest.

When Ben’s eyes glanced down and he sucked in a hard breath, I knew immediately the mistake I made, but I refused to undo it. Stubbornly I stood there and let him gawk at me. I hated that I liked it so much.

“Don’t be like that. We need to talk,” he insisted.

“I have nothing to say to you, Ben. I tried. Lord knows I tried. I wrote you every day and you know how many replies I got back since you finished boot camp? One. One thirty second phone call to say you didn’t want me to come out for your graduation. One letter in nine years, Ben. So, you know what. You can go to hell for all I care.”

That felt really good to get off my chest.

“I’m pretty sure I’ve already been there, Sport, and your letters were the only thing that got me through it.”

The sincerity in his eyes when I dared to look up nearly gutted me.

The front door opened, and my dad peeked his head out. “Honey, Lily apparently appropriated your mom’s last bottle of wine for your last girls’ night. Would you please bail me out and run to the store to grab a bottle?” He startled, as if he had just noticed Ben for the first time. “Benjamin, you’re early.”

“Yes, sir. Sorry, it’s a military habit.” He smiled that smile that had gotten him out of trouble our entire lives.

“Look, Cora will murder me if she knows you’re here and dinner’s not ready. Do me a favor and go with Shelby and we’ll just act like you didn’t know I forgot to pick up the wine,” Dad said.

I wanted to protest, but how? It would just bring up too many questions I didn’t want to answer.

“No problem, sir. Red or white?”

“Red. Thanks so much, both of you.” Dad popped back into the house and shut the door behind him.

I rolled my eyes. "Just wait in your car and I'll be back in a few minutes."

He shrugged and followed me to my car. He was in my passenger seat before I could stop him. I slid into the driver's seat and slammed the door shut.

"I said your car," I grumbled through gritted teeth, knowing he wasn't going to get out.

"I did promise your dad I'd go along with you."

I didn't bother to argue as I drove over to the store to grab a bottle of wine. Ben followed me but didn't say a word. Collier was a small town, though. Of course everyone noticed.

Lotti Moffat was working the register as I got in line to pay.

"I declare it's like time turned back ten years, seeing the two of you together. Benjamin Shay, welcome home. I heard about your daddy. I'm so sorry. If there's anything you all need, please just let us know."

"Thanks, Lotti I appreciate that."

"You must be thrilled to have him home, Shelby."

"Thrilled," I said in a dry voice. I paid and left without another word.

Once in the car, Ben started talking. I wasn't ready to hear it and tried to shush him.

"Do not shush me, Shelbs. I screwed up. I know that now. I was wrong about a lot of things, but especially about you. If I could go back and do it all over again, things would be very different. But I can't. All I can do is start over again."

I didn't respond until I pulled up into the driveway. "You can't just get a do-over, Ben. And I'm not ready to talk to you."

I jumped out of the car before he could respond and ran into the house, barely refraining from slamming the door behind me.

I marched into the kitchen and gave the wine to Mom. Dad quirked a brow at me and I knew he was asking where Ben was. As if to answer his question, there was a knock at the door. Dad grinned and winked at me as he got up to answer it.

"Ben's here," Mom said, clapping her hands together excitedly. "I'm sure the two of you will want to sneak off and catch up, but first, dinner."

I rolled my eyes behind her back and fought not to groan. Of course she'd think that, because I had never let any of my family think a bad thing about Ben or know the extent to which he hurt me.

When Dad came back with Ben in tow, the four of us sat down to dinner. It was awkward for me especially, since no one else seemed to notice or care. I stayed quiet, and even that didn't draw their attention because Ben carried the conversation for everyone.

The hardest part to endure was the images my wolf kept flashing through my mind of Ben and me naked together. *Mine*, she kept growling.

He can't be, I thought.

I was growing uncomfortable and agitated by the moment, then Ben reached his foot across to me and rubbed it against my own under the table. My parents were oblivious to that simple gesture, but the immediate calm it gave me was frightening.

"What's for dessert?" I asked, just trying to speed the evening along.

Mom grinned proudly. "Well, I started to ask Peyton to bake something fabulous, because we all know I'm not that great at it, but then I remembered that your father is supposed to be cutting back on the sweets, and you and Ben used to love that ice cream shop in town and thought it would be great for the two of you to catch up over that instead."

Why did I feel like my parents were trying to set me up with my ex-best friend?

"Tomorrow's Thanksgiving and they probably closed early for it," I said sensibly without straight up protesting the ridiculous idea.

"I had thought about that already, so I called first. They are open until eight tonight. You have plenty of time if you get moving now," Mom said.

"What about the dishes?" I asked.

"Don't be silly, your mother and I can handle that. Go, sweetheart, and have fun. Ben's been gone a long time, and we know how excited you are to see him. We'll be fine," Dad said.

I nearly choked on the sip of water I'd just taken. He couldn't possibly be serious. I tried hard to see it all through his eyes, but I just couldn't. I also couldn't disappoint them, even if it meant spending the remainder of the evening alone with Ben.

Half an hour later we were in Ben's car driving to town. I stared out of the window silently.

"You know this wasn't my idea," he finally said, breaking the silence.

"I know," I said.

"Seriously, Sport, this is the last place on Earth I'd want to go. If there's something else you'd rather do instead, that's okay with me."

My head whipped around towards him and I felt hurt. "Why wouldn't you want to go get milkshakes?" I blurted out.

Ben grimaced in pain. He took a deep breath and gripped the steering wheel so tightly that his knuckles began to turn white.

"I know now, that sack of shit lied to me, and it's taking a lot of control not to drive over to his house and kick his ass, even right now."

"What are you talking about?"

"Grayson's wolf came in right before graduation. He told me that he had bonded with you, that the two of you were true mates."

"And you believed him?" I yelled. He flinched a little at my tone, but I was on the verge of hyperventilating. "Please tell me you didn't do anything stupid because of that."

Ben sunk a little lower in his seat, but kept his eyes fixed on the road.

"Mom asked me to run into town to pick something up after school. I swung by to grab you after your last class, but I saw you and Grayson standing outside your classroom. You were laughing and he put a possessive hand on you and winked at me. He was claiming you in public and you looked happy. I left before I bloodied his nose or did something stupid. I was planning to take you for milkshakes while we were in town. Anyway, it's all a little blurry from there, but I did end up at the ice cream shop, I just couldn't bring myself to walk in without you. I felt empty, like I'd just lost everything I had ever cared about with that one touch I'd witnessed. Somehow I walked in next door instead."

"The Army Recruitment Center," I whispered.

He nodded. "Yeah. I signed up on the spot. I just couldn't bring myself to tell you what I'd done until the last minute. And I'd tried to get you to tell me about you and Grayson, but you wouldn't, and that only made me angrier."

“Because there was nothing to tell,” I reminded him.

“Don’t you think I know that now? For nine years the one thing that got me through it all was the thought that you had found your true mate and were happy. I could live with that, even if it was Grayson Ward.”

“But I wasn’t mated, and I wasn’t happy, Ben. You just left me. You tore out a piece of my heart and took it with you. It’s taken me years to get past all of this and honestly, it’s only been in the last few months that I finally have, and now you’re back and I can’t deal with this.”

“Shelby, I’m not going anywhere,” he said, parking the car in front of one of our favorite places. I couldn’t tell him I hadn’t been back there since the last time I went with him. It held too many memories I didn’t want to face.

“But you are, Ben. You’re home on personal leave because of your dad, but you’re going back. You’ll leave me again and this time, I’m going to be prepared and protect myself from you. It’s best if we just don’t talk or see each other again while you’re home.”

I opened the door and got out. I needed fresh air to breathe that didn’t smell like him. He was out of his door and channeling his wolf speed to reach me before I could even shut the door behind me.

“Are you crazy?” I whispered. “Anyone could see you out here.”

“I don’t care,” he said. “You can’t just run away from this.”

“You mean like you did?” That was low and I knew it, but I would say almost anything to get him to leave again, so that I could begin the long, hard road towards trying to get over Ben Shay once again.

“Shelby, my wolf didn’t surface until a few weeks into Basic. I didn’t know.”

“Know what, Ben?” I asked.

“I didn’t know that you were actually my one true mate,” he practically yelled.

I sucked in a deep breath. Oh God, he felt it, too. I struggled to breathe and had to sit down on the curb to steady myself.

“Shelby? Are you okay? You don’t look so good,” he said, concern filling his voice.

“I’m fine,” I said, a little confused.

My wolf had always known. Of course I'd denied it and thought it was all fabricated from my personal desires, not an actuality. Even when he walked into my classroom and back into my life two days ago, I'd still known who he was to me.

"Don't tell me you didn't know; that you can't feel the call of our bond, too," he said, looking a little worried.

I stared into his eyes and felt the same connection, the same emotions I had always felt for Benjamin Shay. I had loved him my entire life, and nine years apart hadn't changed that one single bit, because he really was my true mate. That reality made my head spin.

"Of course I know that, Ben. I've always known it," I whispered. "I just thought it was wishful thinking, or something on my part; not real."

"Two days ago when I walked into that room to pick up my brothers, I had no idea you would be there. I wasn't even sure if I'd be able to face you, especially when Mom told me you weren't mated yet. But I was blindsided standing there, not just seeing my best friend in the entire world, but my true mate. I didn't have my wolf to guide me before I left, Shelbs. I didn't know. I never could have left you if I had. Never."

All the hurt and anguish came flooding back to me and I started to cry.

"But you did," I managed to say. "You cut me off entirely. You said you loved me, then you walked away and severed everything, even our friendship. Even if I had been mated to someone else, I still needed you in my life. I wasn't ready to face the world alone, to deal with everything. You were gone, Maddie disappeared, I had to . . ." I stopped myself before I blurted out everything. There were some things I just wasn't ready to talk to him about. "It doesn't matter anymore. True mate or not, I'm not sure I can ever trust you again, Ben."

I saw him flinch in physical pain. It hurt me to see it. That was just a sign that our bond was already strengthening. I didn't know what to do. Of course I wanted to fall into his arms and take my happily ever after, but after everything that had happened, I wasn't sure I was strong enough to risk the possible fallout if I did give him a second chance.

"I'll be home for two weeks. Let me prove to you that you can trust me, that I will never let you down or hurt you like that again," he said as he brushed the back of his fingers lightly across my cheek. That simple motion assaulted every one of my senses.

"I can't. I'm not strong enough to resist you, Ben. I need you to just leave me alone," I said honestly.

He grinned and my heart nearly melted at the sight. "I can't and I won't leave you alone, Sport."

I knew he was about to kiss me, and my body sprung to life in anticipation, but I curbed it quickly.

"Two weeks and then what?" I asked. "It was great catching up, but sorry, I have other commitments, maybe I'll see you in another nine years?"

His eyes darkened and he growled low in his chest. "It won't be like that this time."

"Then how will it be, Ben?" I asked.

He sighed and looked away, then straight into my eyes. "I was shot in the back. It nicked my spine and the doctors know it. I've been benched, despite the fact my accelerated healing has mended it just fine. I am bound to an electric chair pretending to be temporarily paralyzed. It sucks ass, but my major goes out of his way to make sure my unit flies under the radar. He protects us and maintains our most important secrets. I'm not sure how to get out of this situation, and neither is he, because the type of injury I sustained isn't typically recoverable for a human."

I couldn't believe what he was telling me. "The army knows what you are?" I blurted out, scared for him and all of us. Humans couldn't handle the truth about us.

He nodded. "I'm part of an elite special forces unit. We're all the same," he said cryptically because we weren't in an area where it was safe to talk. "It's safe, Shelbs. I promise you. It's just going to take some finagling to work through the paper trail and doctor reports on this one. Because of this I haven't signed my re-up papers yet. I can sign on for another three to five years. There's a fantastic bonus included in that. Or I can choose not to and I'm out, likely with a full medical discharge even. I do have to return for a couple weeks, maybe a month to get things sorted, but I'm not committed to staying there forever. I can come home, Shelby. We can be together, start over, settle down, raise a family, everything we always dreamed of. It's a second chance for the both of us."

My heart soared, then crashed to the ground. I couldn't give him everything he wanted. Our childhood hopes and dreams had been shattered years before. Still, the look in his eyes had me biting my tongue. I couldn't burst his blissful bubble with reality. For the first time since he returned I felt like I was truly looking at my Ben.

"How about that ice cream?" I asked, avoiding the situation entirely.

Ben

Chapter 10

It was a start, I thought as I helped her to her feet and escorted her into the ice cream shop.

The man behind the counter stopped and stared. A big smile spread across his face.

"Why, I haven't seen the two of you around here in ages. Benjamin, welcome home. It's great to see you two together again. Shelby, you must be mighty proud of him."

She smiled and gave a non-committal nod.

"Mr. Elder, it's great to see you again," I said.

"Just Graham, son. I was army, too, you know."

I smiled warmly. "I didn't. Thank you for you service."

"And the same to you. Milkshakes are on the house," he said.

"That's not necessary," Shelby told him.

"When one of our own comes home without a visible wound, it's my honor to welcome him back, Shelby. This is the least I can do."

"Thank you, sir," I said, before Shelby could protest further. I had learned early on that although humbling, it was important to let others show their thanks for our serving, as they felt called to do. Arguing only made you come across as an ungrateful ass. For every person who had bestowed me kindness, I purposefully returned in kind as soon as possible. It may have been as simple as paying for the car behind me going through the drive thru or stopping to help a kid find his ball. Whatever opportunity presented itself I took it, and honestly my job saw entirely too much darkness in this world. Both receiving and spreading a bit of thanks kept me grounded in the light over the years.

"Cherry for you Shelby, and chocolate for Lieutenant Shay. Did I get that title right? How about those drinks? Memory's not always so great these days," he said.

"Spot on for both, sir," I assured him.

We waited by the counter until our milkshakes were ready, then I directed Shelby back to the corner booth we had always sat in.

She had been stiff ever since my bold speech about quitting the army and coming home to her. I'd meant every word of it. Now that I knew without a doubt that Shelby was meant to be mine, I would do everything in my power to be here for her and put a smile on her face every single day of the rest of her life. I still wasn't sure it would make up for the last nine years we'd missed out on, but it was a start.

I decided to switch tactics and not directly push things for now.

"Dad's apparently having another surgery tomorrow. Mom's leaving in the morning to spend some time with him, but the boys and I aren't going until Friday morning. Your mother had previously invited them to Thanksgiving dinner with your family. That was before anyone knew I was coming home, but that offer has been extended to me as well. I'll take your lead on this, Sport, just tell me what to do here."

She took a long sip from her milkshake and sighed. She reached for mine as if on autopilot and took a drink from it, too. I didn't think she even realized she was doing it. Shelby loved chocolate-cherry anything, but when it came to milkshakes, she claimed the combination was too rich, so she always ordered a cherry vanilla shake and then chased it with my chocolate one.

"Of course you and the boys should come to dinner," she finally said.

I fought down the grin threatening to spread across my face. It felt like my first real breakthrough with her since my return.

"You're sure?"

She rolled her eyes. "I'd tell you if I wasn't," she said.

It was true. Feelings be damned, Shelby had always been open and honest with me.

"I know you would," I said. "I was just double-checking. And thanks. I'm sure it will help the twins take their minds off of Dad's surgery."

She reached across the table and squeezed my hand. "I really am sorry about your dad, Ben. And I can't believe they are doing surgery on Thanksgiving."

Her sincerity coupled by the powerful emotions that jolted through me like I'd just been struck by lightning when she touched me were almost too much to bear.

"Thanks," I managed to say. "Apparently it's an emergency need and they didn't want to put it off any longer. We just found out today."

"How are you holding up?" she asked.

I shrugged. "So far I haven't let it be real, if you know what I mean."

"Staying disconnected? Unattached?"

"Exactly. Basic survival 101," I admitted.

"It's okay to feel, you know," she said, sounding worried about me.

I really liked that she cared enough to worry. It gave me hope that things would work out okay for us.

"I feel plenty, Shelby. I'm not entirely numb to the situation, just enough to function through the tough days. It's a little harder to do here than it was in the field."

"Because of your family?" she asked.

I shook my head. "No, Sport, because of you."

I didn't feel bad about being honest, but I did nearly chuckle because she'd walked right into that. She took another sip of her milkshake, and then mine. She frowned and stared down at my cup in her hand before passing it back.

"Sorry," she muttered.

"Don't be. I always order chocolate just for you," I confessed.

"What? I thought it was your favorite."

I shook my head. "Nah, It's only my favorite when I'm with you, because I love watching you steal it. Always have. I'm actually more of a cookies and cream kind of guy," I admitted. Shelby was the one person in this world that knew more about me than even I did at times, but she didn't know everything.

"That's impossible. How many shakes have we shared in our lifetime? Thousands probably and you always, always, always order chocolate."

I laughed. "That's because you used to torment yourself between ordering the cherry or the chocolate, claiming they were too rich together. You'd always order the cherry but wish you'd gotten the chocolate, so it just became my default order with you, always chocolate. I like it the best of those two, but I liked taking that stress off you and watching you just enjoy your shake more."

I could see the confusion on her face and knew she was thinking back through every milkshake we'd ever shared together.

She was quiet, contemplative as we finished our shakes and got up to leave.

"Thanks a lot, Graham," I said on our way out.

I held the door open for Shelby out of old habit. It seemed crazy how those little gestures felt so effortless with her. As if on its own accord, my hand gently rested on her lower back to guide her back to my car. Immediate peace washed over me from touching her like that, and my wolf settled at the possessive gesture.

Shelby stiffened, but didn't move. I helped her into the car then ran around to jump into the driver's seat. On the way home, I reached to hold her hand. She nearly jumped away from me, as far to the other side of the car as possible, and then pulled her hand away as if I had just burned her. An internal searing pain I'd never felt before jabbed me inside my chest. I immediately realized it was the pain of rejection.

"You can't keep touching me, Ben," she said.

"I can't help it," I admitted. "My wolf is going crazy and it's the only thing that settles him."

If it was anyone else I would have eagerly pursued my mate until the bond was sealed, but this was Shelby. We had so much history and thanks to me being a teenage bonehead, not all of it was good.

I knew I had hurt her, and I'd have to live with that knowledge for the rest of my life, but until I came home and saw her for myself, I could never have realized just how badly I'd hurt her by leaving the way I had.

At first I had tried to keep in touch. I returned a few of her letters during boot camp when I needed to hold onto home, not ready to let go. As I settled into a new life without Shelby though, it was just a constant reminder of what I was missing.

I wrote her one final letter to just let her know I was okay when I received my first deployment orders. She kept writing me every single day. Some days they were painful to look at knowing how much of her life I was missing out on. It wasn't until they stopped arriving that I clung to them for survival.

The thing was, I'd always confided in Shelby, but I had no idea how to tell her that I was still madly in love with her and always had been. I didn't know how to say she was the only girl for me and that I'd remained faithful to her all these years, even while believing she belonged to someone else.

I didn't know how to tell my best friend that I missed her so much that I would give up absolutely everything I'd built for myself just to be with her.

The words were right there on the tip of my tongue, but I couldn't say them. It wasn't a shocker that our wolves were falling into perfect sync. I could read her emotions like an open book even when we were kids, but I could actually feel them now after just spending a few hours with her.

She was still upset and scared. I didn't know how to fix that

"Sport, talk to me, please. I need to know what you're thinking. I get you're not happy about this, but we're mating, Shelbs."

"I don't know what to say to you, Ben. If you had come home even two months ago, I probably would have tossed everything aside and run to you with open arms, but I've been working through a lot of shit lately and I'm finally in a good place...honestly, for the first time since before you left."

I blew out a breath. Things here had been worse than I thought. I understood now why Troy was so angry with me.

"It's Walker, isn't it? Your boyfriend?" I asked.

She looked surprised. "Who told you about Walker?"

"Your mother. She's quite fond of him," I admitted through gritted teeth. "I get you weren't burning the candle waiting for me to come home, Sport, but now that I'm here, I'll kill him if he lays a hand on you. You are mine," I said more aggressively than I meant.

She was quiet, and that was never a good sign. Her phone dinged, breaking the silence. It had been doing that off and on all day and she genuinely smiled every time.

I watched in my peripheral vision as she returned the text, smiled, and set the phone back in her lap. Two seconds later it chimed again. This time she laughed.

"Sorry," she said.

"Does he know about me?" I asked.

She put the phone down and looked at me. "Of course he does. He finds our current situation hysterical. And you can tame down the macho shit. Walker and I aren't even together. We went out on a couple dates while he was in town with Maddie a couple months ago. We both knew there was nothing there, but we did become good friends."

"Did you kiss him?" I asked.

"Not your business, but yes."

I growled. It was deep and low and surprised me.

"Did you sleep with him?"

Shelby scowled. "Ben, that's none of your business. You weren't around, you have no right to ask or judge. Maybe I did, maybe I didn't."

My shoulders slouched as I was slammed by the feelings of betrayal. I gripped the steering wheel hard enough to leave handprints and drove a little faster to get us home. I needed a break from Shelby. Everything was too overwhelming and the thought of her with another man was tearing me up inside.

"Hey, Ben, slow down," she said.

Her hand went to my shoulder and rubbed on the tense muscles there. It started to calm me, and I pulled over to the side of the road to regain some control.

"Look at me, Ben," she said.

I didn't want to because I knew she could see the hurt and betrayal I felt. But I forced myself to anyway. This was Shelby, my mate. There was no one else on Earth I would let myself be this vulnerable with.

She sighed and pulled her hand from me. She wrung them in her lap as she stared at the floor.

"I didn't sleep with Walker," she said softly. "I haven't been with anyone like that since you left. Only you."

The relief and possession that washed over me was all-consuming. I was out of the car and opening her door before I could process what was happening. I carefully unbuckled her seat belt and pulled her out.

"Ben, what are you. . ." she managed to say before I pinned her against the car with my body and kissed her.

I expected her to go stiff in my arms and need a little coaxing, but the second our lips touch she responded with a hunger equal to my own. I put my hands on her ass and lifted her higher, so we were equal in height. Her legs naturally wrapped around my waist.

As her most intimate parts pressed against mine, I immediately hardened. I felt instant relief. Over the years the guys had tried to hook me up with numerous girls but just couldn't go through with it. I had wondered if there was something physically wrong with me, or if I was just struggling with guilt, pining over a woman I didn't think I could ever have. As far as I was concerned, this proved the latter was my problem, only now I knew I could have her.

We were both breathing heavily when she started to slow our kisses. If she hadn't, I might have marked her right there in the open for anyone passing by to see.

"Ben, this is crazy," she finally said.

I kissed her again, more gently this time. I knew she was still fragile and would be more vulnerable with the heightened emotions passing between us.

I rested my head against her forehead. "I have so much I want to say to you, to tell you, but I'm terrified you're going to vanish in my arms."

She hugged me tightly and we stayed that way for an undetermined amount of time.

"You said I have two weeks. There's no point in rushing nine years into day one," she said as she unwrapped her legs from around me and slid back to the ground.

I smiled and nodded. "Fair enough. I can still bring the twins over for Thanksgiving tomorrow, right?"

She nodded and even smiled.

"And you'll actually be there, right? I don't need to show up an hour early to catch you making a run for the hills, do I?"

She pushed at my chest. “I’m not running from you, Ben.”

Shelby

Chapter 11

When I walked into the house, my head was swimming. Ben had escorted me to the front door and kissed me goodnight. He still took my breath away, but I was terrified he'd leave in two weeks and I'd never hear from him again, mated or not. Knowing we were true mates and feeling our bond growing by the minute made me even more scared. I had witnessed what an unresolved bond looked like, and I didn't think I was strong enough to live through it.

Maddie was still up rocking Sara in the living room, though the rest of the house was quiet because it was late. Ben and I had gone down to the river and sat and talked some. I had a better picture of what he had been doing all these years and I'd admitted the struggles I'd had seeking out a career. Neither of us talked about anything too personal, but it was nice.

"Hey, Cora and Zach were making bets on how late you'd be out. They just went up to bed," Maddie said.

"Hey, you're here!" I said. "When did you guys get in?"

"About an hour ago. Oscar was tired so he and Liam went straight to bed, but this one was ready to party," she said, looking down affectionately at her daughter.

Maddie and I had been close once. I was the first to open up to her and accept her back. She'd asked me to be at her wedding, to which of course I'd said yes. Still, in the last two years of having her back in our lives, we hadn't really talked about stuff.

"Do you want to talk about it?" she asked. "Lily filled me in a little over the phone. Ben left nine years ago, and you really haven't heard from him since. Now he's back, that's got to be hard, or is this a good thing?"

I shrugged again. "Jury's still out."

"Well, you looked happy when you walked in, if that's any consolation."

"It's pretty surreal having him back here," I said.

"I know from our girls' night last time I was here that you and he were pretty close. Are those old feelings resurfacing?" she asked. "Because you're blushing like a girl who just had the best sex of her life or who just met her one true mate."

"We didn't have sex," I blurted out, unable to deny the other.

Maddie's mouth dropped open, then she closed it as she contemplated what to say next. It clearly did not go unnoticed that I didn't deny the second accusation. I just couldn't. I needed to tell someone.

"Um, do you want to talk about it?" she finally asked. "Because if you're saying what I think you're saying, that's a pretty big deal, Shelbs."

"I think I've always known, Maddie," I confessed. "It doesn't feel like some big revelation, but there are things I should have told him, and I didn't because I was so mad at him at the time. What if he can't forgive me? I've barely forgiven myself."

She nodded. "If anyone can understand and appreciate that, it's me. You think I wanted Liam to know about everything that happened to me? I didn't think he could forgive me everything I had done, even knowing that most of it wasn't my fault. But he needed to know for us to move past it, for me to move past it."

I sighed. I knew what I needed to do, but it would wait until after Thanksgiving.

"Oh, not to completely change the subject on you, but Cora wanted me to tell you that since dinner at Peyton's went so well last time, she caved and is moving Thanksgiving there, too. Something about the kitchen being nicer to cook in."

"Mom's letting Peyton host Thanksgiving?" I asked, shocked to hear it.

"Apparently it's a group effort with just a location change," Maddie said with a laugh. "But basically, yeah. She wanted me to tell you to let Ben know, said he and his brothers were supposed to be having dinner with us."

I pulled out my phone and frowned down at it. "I don't have his number," I confessed. "I can try the house."

It rang four times and I was about to hang up when Will answered. "Shay residence."

I could hear Troy and Ben yelling in the background but could only make out some of it.

"I told you to stay the hell away from her," Troy said.

"I can't, Troy. Someday you'll understand, but I can't."

"You're just going to leave again, Ben, and then we'll all be left to clean up your mess. She deserves better."

"Probably, but that's not how this works," Ben said.

"Hello?" Will asked and I realized I hadn't said anything.

"Hey, Will, it's Shelby. Can I speak with Ben?"

"Um, yeah. You can probably hear it's not the best time, but I'll try," he laughed. He muffled the phone with his hand. "Ben, Shelby's on the phone."

"Did she just hear all that?" Troy demanded.

"Probably. I think the whole Pack heard you two," Will said.

"Hello?" Ben said, taking the phone from Will.

"Hey," I said, awkwardly feeling like I was eavesdropping.

"I don't know how much of that you caught, but I'm sorry. Troy's quite protective of you."

"He's a great kid, Ben. I'll talk to him tomorrow. I've heard mating males struggle enough without Troy being territorial, too."

"I'll handle it," he said.

"Whatever," I said, not wanting to fight about it and having already made my mind up to pull Troy aside and talk tomorrow. "I'm calling because you didn't give me your cell number, and Mom wanted me to tell you that Thanksgiving has been moved to Peyton's house."

"Okay, address?"

I spouted it off. "I can pick you up on my way if you want to head over early? That's up to you."

"That won't be too weird?" he asked.

"Oh, I have no doubt things are going to get weird. Peyton hates you by the way. That alone—weird."

"Why does Peyton hate me?" he asked.

"Because you hurt me, dummy," I said. "She's my big sister and was here for much of the fallout. Plus, she's the only one I confide in, though she'll probably get mad at me when she finds out I talked to Maddie about you first."

He laughed. "I dropped you off like twenty minutes ago and you're already talking it out with your sister?"

I smiled. "She was up with the baby, so yeah. I needed it. In some ways she and I aren't so different after all."

"You sound okay, so I'm glad you talked to her."

"I'm fine, Ben."

"I'm not," he confessed. "I'd feel a whole lot better if you weren't out of my sight. You could just come over and stay here for the night," he offered.

"You know that wouldn't be appropriate with your brothers there," I said with a laugh.

"Fine. I'll see you tomorrow then. Go ahead and pick us up, it'll give me more time with you," he surprised me by saying, especially since I already warned him that Peyton wouldn't be happy to see him.

"I did offer that, but I'm expected there by eight, and something tells me that Will and Troy will not be happy to wake up that early on their holiday break."

I could hear his smile reaching his voice when he replied. "They'll get over it. Besides, Mom is leaving early in the morning, so we'll be up."

"Fine. I'll see you in the morning," I said.

"Sweet dreams, Sport," he replied.

I wanted to tell him that I loved him, but I hesitated then just hung up the phone.

When I headed off to bed there were a million things running through my head, so I reached into my nightstand and pulled out my stationery. I started writing a new letter to Ben, even though I had said I wouldn't do that ever again. This time it was different, though. When I finished and sealed it, I went to my closet, dumped out a new pair of shoes I had recently bought and put the new letter in the box. It felt like a fresh start.

As I climbed back into bed, I fell fast asleep with a big smile on my face.

The alarm clock sounded off far too early. I groaned. I'd set it an hour early so I could shower and shave and make myself more presentable than usual, even knowing my family would call me out on it. It wasn't like we could hide the fact that Ben and I were true mates anyway.

I still didn't know what to do about everything that was happening, and I didn't trust he would even stay in touch once he left, but he asked me to give him two weeks, and I owed it to the both of us to see that through with an open heart.

The weirdest thing was that with Ben back, it was harder to remember the bad times. I was too overcome by the good memories of growing up with my best friend and our dreams for the future that felt so tangible now. It saddened me that I couldn't give him everything we'd ever dreamed about, but that was my life, and he'd have to decide if he could live with it or not.

I wasn't going to let that dampen the day, though. I had always loved Thanksgiving and having all my family together. This year everyone would truly be there and that deserved a celebration.

After carefully blowing out my hair and applying makeup, I chose a pretty yellow dress that complemented my brown hair and made my brown eyes pop. It was fitted in all the right places but flared at the bottom, so I didn't feel like my thighs were being confined. Pretty and functional, it was perfect for the day. I paired it with some brown leggings and matching brown boots. Grabbing my jacket, I headed for the door.

I arrived at Ben's at exactly eight o'clock. I was nervous, but not about Ben. I was nervous about the boys. Had he already told them?

I took a deep breath, got out of the vehicle, and walked to the door. I knocked and waited.

To my surprise, his mother answered the door. "Marnie," I said, reaching to hug her. "I'm so sorry about everything. Are you okay?" I asked.

"No, but I will be. Fortunately, it's his left leg, and as long as they keep him drugged, I only feel mild pain in mine, though the actual accident and before they got his pain under control was unbearable if I'm being honest."

Ben's parents were fully bonded. That meant they could experience things together that only bonded pairs could, including sharing pain. And if he had died in that accident, Marnie would have, too. It's said to be a blessing more than the curse it sounds like.

"Are you sure you'll be okay to drive? The boys can blow off Thanksgiving. Heck, I will too and drive you myself if you need me to," I offered, unsure what else to say or do.

"Don't be silly, Shelby. I'm fine, and even better knowing my boys will have a good Thanksgiving. He'll be in surgery all day today and they have a bed for me to help with additional pain, if I require it. He'll be out, but it may not knock me out. We'll see. I know he's in good hands and Thomas is taking care of everything, including flying me out there so I don't have to drive. It's far more than we could have asked for," she assured me.

"Well, if there's anything at all I can do, please just ask."

She smiled at me. "You're taking care of my boys today and letting them be a part of your family's celebration. Be sure to thank Cora for me. I really appreciate her inviting them. I didn't want them sitting around the hospital all day on Thanksgiving."

I nodded. "I'll be sure they have a good time. Maddie's in town. Her son Oscar is close to the twins' age. I'm sure they'll have a great time."

She shifted her eyes back into the house and dropped her voice. "Are you certain you're okay with Ben being there?" I loved that his mother was worried about me. "I know how difficult it was on you after he left for the army and I know he stopped keeping in touch with you. I don't understand why, but I can imagine how much harder that was on you. I'm worried about him spending time with you while he's home, knowing he'll be going back in a few weeks."

I sighed. I knew it was going to be hard, but what choice did I have? He was my true mate. "I'm a big girl now, Marnie. I'll deal with it. You don't need to worry about me."

Ben opened the door. "Mom, I thought you left already." He looked down at his watch. "Sport, you're late."

"I was right on time. I'm just talking to your mom."

"Oh yeah, about what?"

"Nothing," Marnie and I said at the same time.

"Why does that scare the shit out of me?"

"Language, Ben. You're not in the Navy, no need to talk like a sailor," she reminded him.

"Sorry, Mom," he said with a sheepish grin.

"Alright, I'm going to hit the road. Behave today, you and the twins," she warned.

He gave his mom a kiss goodbye on the cheek, then as she walked away from us, he risked giving me a quick kiss on the lips.

"You look beautiful," he said, making me blush.

"I said behave, Ben. Stop flirting with Shelby. You're lucky she's even talking to you," Marnie warned.

"Bye, Mom," he said. "Troy, Will, our ride's here. Let's go."

Ben

Chapter 12

My foot wouldn't stop bouncing as we drove to Peyton's. I was a nervous wreck. I never got nervous. Being a sniper meant I was incapable of feeling nerves and if I did, I risked death. It was that simple.

I hadn't told Shelby what I did in the military. I had killed people. How would she feel about that when she found out?

"Why are you so jumpy?" Will asked.

"Because he knows my sister will not be happy to see him," Shelby informed him.

I groaned.

"Why?" Troy asked. I knew if he could shoot laser beams from his eyes, I'd already be dead. I could feel him staring holes into the back of my head since he climbed into the back seat of Shelby's car.

"Because I was an ass about how I left things here. You already know this, Troy. You've been giving me shit for it since the moment I got back," I reminded him.

I imagined his eyes were about to bug out his head that I'd had the audacity to say that in front of Shelby. I hadn't told them she was my true mate. I didn't want to share that with even my family until I knew it was okay with her.

"Peyton can be a little overprotective of those she cares about," Shelby said.

"Good. I hope she rips his throat out," Troy said under his breath.

Shelby pulled the car over to the side of the road and put it into park, then turned to look at Troy. "You don't mean that, Troy."

"Yes, I do. I remember. I remember how he just left without any warning. I remember how much Mom cried for days and how worried she is all the time, wondering if we'll ever hear from him again. And I remember you crying too, Ms. Shelby. He hurt you too, not just us. You and Ben were inseparable just like Will and Caroline are now, and then he was just gone. Everyone thinks we were too young to remember, but I remember everything."

I hated hearing him talk like that. It was ripping a hole in my heart that I'd kept bandaged for years. Logically I knew I would hurt them all by my actions, but in order to survive, I'd had to push all that down and forget it. If I'd lived life with that much guilt hanging over me, I'd never have survived Basic, let alone nine years as a Ghost.

"Troy," I started, but Shelby raised her hand and cut me off.

"Listen, both of you," she said. "Yes, I was hurt and upset when Ben left the way he did, but he did what he needed to do to get through a rough time in his life. It wasn't personal. It may have felt like it was, but it wasn't. Ben loves you guys, and he loves your parents, too. He would never knowingly hurt any of you like that. My issues were just that, mine. And I'm okay. It's all made me so much stronger. Troy, you can't live life with all this pent-up anger towards him though. Trust me, it's not healthy."

"But. . ." Troy tried to interject, but Shelby cut him off, too.

"No buts, Troy." She took a deep breath and stared at me for a moment before reaching for my hand. "There's also something you both need to know and try to understand. When Ben left here he was barely eighteen. His wolf hadn't come in yet, but mine had and she was very much set on him. There were some other factors, but that's basically why it was so much harder on me than it should have been."

I hated hearing her talk like that. I squeezed her hand.

"My wolf hadn't come in and I thought she had mated with someone else. It was a big misunderstanding that I'll likely regret every day of the rest of my life. I didn't know when I left that Shelby was my one true mate."

Troy gasped and Will laughed.

"You're serious?"

Shelby turned to look at me and smiled, really smiled for probably the first time since I got home.

"Yeah, he's serious," she confirmed. "We've got a lot of crap to deal with now, and it would be a lot easier if you backed off him a bit, Troy. I really appreciate you looking out for me, but this isn't something we can just ignore."

"I didn't know," he whispered.

"I know you didn't, and aside from the two of you, only my sister Maddie knows about this. Can you two keep it between us for now? Just until we figure out what the hell we're doing," she said, making them both laugh.

"Yeah, we can do that," Will said, elbowing his twin who finally nodded. "Thanks for trusting us with this."

The tension in the car was lifted as Shelby turned back in her seat and continued the drive. Peyton lived in a big old house just outside Collier territory. As I rode along, Shelby told me how her sister had mated a Larken wolf and they'd bought the original Collier house and fixed it up. Since it had been sold off decades ago, it wasn't considered Collier territory any longer. Peyton had put the house in both her and her mate, Oliver's, names to ensure neither pack could claim it, giving her family a safe neutral zone to live in.

She also told me how Oliver had come with a ready-made family of three brothers that he had raised practically on his own and an infant daughter named Eve. She went on to say that Ruby also had taken a mate named Bran, and they had a baby girl named Opal. Maddie had mated Liam Westin and they had two kids, Oscar and Sara. Lizzy and Clara were both happily mated, but no kids, and Thomas had taken Lily Collier as a mate.

"Lily is dying to have a baby, but Thomas isn't ready," Shelby said as she concluded her family's history over the last few years. "Oh, and Oscar is about your age, guys. I think you'll have fun with him today."

"Cool," Will said.

I was pretty certain both the boys had already tuned her out and had no idea who Oscar was.

"And everyone's in for Thanksgiving?" I asked, starting to feel slightly intimidated.

"Yup. The entire family," she confirmed as we pulled up in front of a big white house.

The four of us got out in no real hurry to get this day started.

"Come on, let's get this over with," she said.

I reached for her hand and pulled her to me, giving her a long hug before walking into the lion's den.

"Five dollars says they announce it before desserts been served," Will said to Troy.

"You're on. I say someone's going to ask before the turkey's carved. It's so obvious," Troy told him.

Shelby groaned as I leaned down and kissed the top of her head.

"We can do this. Should have taken them up on that bet," I said, making her laugh.

"You can't keep your hands off me for even a full minute, I'd place my bet with Troy."

"I can behave, just wait and see," I told her even though I knew she was right. At least everyone there was happily mated and not a threat. I could get through it without drawing suspicions.

Peyton met us at the door. She looked me over and scowled.

"Ben," she said.

"Peyton," I replied politely even as I felt the tension starting to rise.

"Why the hell is he here this early?" She looked out into the driveway and immediately noticed only Shelby's car was there. "And why the hell did he ride with you?"

"Not today Peyton, please," Shelby begged.

Peyton sighed. "Come on in," she finally relented.

Apparently we weren't the first ones to arrive. Shelby hugged a young boy that I guessed was Oscar. She confirmed it when she introduced my brothers to him.

"The babies are in the playroom, if you want to stop in and say hi," Peyton said, giving me a smirk that made me feel very uncomfortable.

"Sure, come meet my nieces," Shelby told me as she started to reach for my hand, but jerked it back when she remembered.

Before we even walked into the room, my wolf jumped into high alert. I'd always trusted his instincts and immediately moved to protect my mate.

"What's wrong?" she asked.

"I'm not sure yet," I confessed.

Shelby just laughed and pushed me to the side to walk into the room anyway.

"Walker," she squealed, launching herself into another man's arms.

I couldn't hold in the growl that erupted from me. Shelby turned to chastise me for it.

"Hi, you must be Ben," he said, and Shelby blushed.

My eyes shot to hers with so many questions, but she just shrugged.

"Ben, this is Walker," she said, stepping away from him and discreetly putting her hand on my arm. It started to calm my wolf, but I still had a lot of questions.

I immediately started to size the man up. He was tall, almost as big as me, and too handsome for my liking. I could take him in a fight, but I suspected Shelby wouldn't be happy if I messed up that too pretty face of his.

"Why didn't you tell me you were coming?" she asked.

He shrugged and smiled. "Wanted to surprise you."

My eyes shot back to hers, but she just shook her head.

"Walker travels with Maddie and Liam, or more so my niece and nephew. He's assigned to their security detail."

"Security, huh?" I asked.

"Yeah, I'm with Westin Force's Delta team," he said proudly. "This is just one of my jobs."

"Babysitting seems like a promising career," I mumbled under my breath.

Shelby elbowed me and shot me a look to tell me she was not happy with my comment. Walker seemed completely unaffected by it.

He shrugged easily. "Not my first choice, but we take the assignments we're handed without argument. Shelby tells me you're in the army, so I'm sure you know what that's like. She didn't mention what it was you do exactly."

Normally I would bullshit something and downplay my role, but my heightened testosterone had me wanting to put this punk in his place.

"I'm a sniper with one of the Ranger teams," I said proudly, not able to bring myself to admit I was a Ghost. If this guy had any military knowledge whatsoever, and I suspected he did, then he'd know exactly what that was, but my guys were still out there doing what we do, and I would never jeopardize their safety by admitting to that.

"Sniper, huh? Talk to Cole Anderson if you're considering getting out of the army, I hear there's an opening for a guy with your particular skillset," Walker said, surprising me. "Shelby and I are just friends, man. I just want her to be happy."

"I'm aware," I said dryly, still not sure what to think of this guy. "You're also the only unmated male I've encountered here, so forgive me if I'm not ready to make friendship bracelets."

Walker started laughing and slapped me on the shoulder. "Warning heard, loud and clear."

He knows? I mouthed to Shelby.

She shrugged and hung her head in embarrassment. "He's sort of like my current best friend, Ben. I tell him just about everything. Sorry," she said, but I knew she wasn't really.

"You replaced me with him?" I asked.

Walker laughed. "Don't think of it like that. Think of it as you've been upgraded to a higher status I will never achieve."

I didn't want to like Walker, but it was kind of hard not to. The man certainly had balls of steal for talking so openly with me like that.

As Shelby leaned down and picked up a curly-headed little girl, I froze and just watched her. She looked so natural as she cuddled the child and made her smile. My heart swelled. I knew how badly Shelby had always wanted to be a mom and I couldn't wait to give that to her. With a final kiss on the top of her sweet little head, Shelby placed the child back into the playpen she had found her in and stood to stretch.

"I've got work to do. You two play nice together, please? For me," she said.

"We'll be fine," Walker assured her.

I still wasn't as certain.

I didn't see Shelby again for a few hours. She was kept hostage working in the kitchen with the other women. There was lots of talking and giggling. The sounds of happiness filled the house.

Walker and I found a spot in the front living room and sat and talked. Damned if I didn't like the guy. He told me a little more about Westin Force and some of the things they were doing there. When Lizzy and Cole Anderson arrived, Walker snagged him to explain even further just why a wolf pack would need the talents of a sniper.

"While we have security and sharpshooters on every Force unit, it's the Bravo team that acts as our ultimate protection. They're the only unit I know of that would seek out a sniper," Cole informed me.

"Bravo? Not Alpha?" I asked out of curiosity.

Cole laughed. "Kyle has a thing about no unit being ranked equal or higher than him, so as the Alpha, there can't be an actual Alpha unit. Likewise, he holds two Betas, so instead of Beta company, they were dubbed Bravo."

"Sounds pretty intense over there. May I ask why all of this is necessary?"

Cole shrugged. "You'd be surprised, Ben. Elise and Lily have both been kidnapped. There have been multiple threats on Kyle's mate, Kelsey's, life. There are some underlying concerns for shifter-kind that they are sorting through. I can't really go into detail as that's all classified, but Westin Force goes far beyond just protecting Westin Pack, it's in place to protect and serve all shifters."

"Have you heard of the Ghosts?" I asked.

"Who hasn't? Rumors have it that particular Army Rangers unit is comprised of all shifters," Walker piped in.

"It is," Cole confirmed. "Why do you ask?"

"How do you guys know that?" I wondered aloud.

Cole grinned. "There's not much that gets past our guys. We make it a point to know everything there is to know, who our opposition may be, and where our allies stand. Silas Granger runs our Bravo team. He's been looking for an in to recruit from the Ghosts for a long time, but they always elude him. Drives him batshit crazy. There's definitely a reason they call themselves the Ghosts. We thrive ourselves on having state-of-the-art technology and the highest intelligence in the world, but those guys are second to none."

"Tell me, how much travel does the Force require?" I asked.

Walker shrugged. "Depends on the position and the jobs that arise. For me, I spend ninety percent or more of the time at home. Silas's team is less, maybe seventy-five percent of their time. They always get the coolest missions."

"And he's definitely looking for a sniper?" I asked.

Cole looked at Walker.

"That's the word around base," Walker confirmed.

"Can you set me up a meeting with him before I head back?" I asked.

"Ben, you seem like a great guy, but these guys are hardcore. They only seek out the best of the best," Cole warned.

I didn't mean to sound cocky or toot my horn when I replied, "I am the best of the best, and if he's looking for an in to recruit from the Ghosts, I know people," I said, still refusing to confirm I was one.

"No one just knows people when it comes to the Ghosts," Walker challenged. "You'd have to be . . ." He stopped mid-sentence, as if the pieces I'd laid out for him finally clicked into place.

Changing the subject quickly, I turned back to Cole. "Are any of the Bravo unit mated?"

"What? Why?" he asked.

"Just answer the question," Walker told him.

"One, I think, why?"

"Because I'm looking for a change that will keep me employed but still allow plenty of time at home."

"With your mate," Walker finished for me.

I didn't confirm or deny it as I stared Cole down.

"Patrick O'Connell oversees the program. That would be a better question to ask him, but I can put you in touch and if he's interested after you speak to him—and I can't imagine that he wouldn't be—he'll also be able to arrange a meeting with Silas. How long are you home for?"

"Another eleven days," I said. "And I cannot use it all on this."

He nodded. "I heard about your father. I'm really sorry."

Lizzy and Shelby walked into the room laughing. When I looked up, all seriousness faded from my face and morphed into a smile. I couldn't help it. Shelby looked so beautiful, she took my breath away every time I looked at her.

"Benjamin Shay," Lizzy said, shaking her head. "Welcome home."

"Thanks, Lizzy. It's good to be home."

"I see you've already met my mate," she exclaimed, leaning down to give Cole a quick kiss.

I somehow refrained from saying, "I see you've found mine as well." Instead, I discreetly winked at Shelby.

Cole's phone rang and he grinned down at it. "Speak of the devil." He turned his phone for Walker and me to see it was Patrick calling. "I'll take this outside, and let you know what he says."

"Thank you," I told him.

Lizzy excused herself and headed back to the kitchen, but Shelby stuck around. She sat down on the coffee table in front of us and demanded to know what was going on.

"What was that all about?" she asked.

"Hooking your boy up with a new job," Walker said. "How do you feel about Westin Pack?"

Her face fell as she gave me a serious look. "You're serious?"

"I'm just looking into my options, Sport. There's not exactly a ton of jobs requiring my particular expertise. They may have one. I'm not making any decisions without you," I assured her. "I'm just seeing what's out there."

"You were serious when you said you'd leave the military?" she asked.

I reached over and took both her hands in mine, not caring who saw us. "Shelbs, this isn't my life, this is our life now. We'll figure out what's best for us, okay?"

She had tears in her eyes as she gave me a hesitant smile and nodded.

Shelby

Chapter 13

As I helped finish the last of our Thanksgiving meal, my mind was a million miles away. I had been proceeding with caution where Ben was concerned, but he seemed serious about getting out of the military. I wasn't going to ask him to do that. I could handle him being away, as long as he didn't go dark on me again or never come back home.

I hadn't even considered what other options there may be for us. I just started my new career and loved it. Could I pack up and leave Collier?

San Marco was nice, and I would have Maddie there, plus half the year I'd have Lizzy, too. I loved the Westins, but could I call it home?

I wasn't sure and I knew that I wasn't going to figure it all out today. I tried to push the thoughts aside, but it was hard.

"You look a million miles away," Mom commented.

"Sorry, just a lot on my mind," I admitted.

"Walker and Ben seem to be hitting it off. I'll be honest, I was a little nervous about having the two of them here together."

"Why?" I asked.

Mom gave me a stern look. "You are not that oblivious, Shelby. Anyone can see Ben still has feelings for you."

"They can?"

She shot me another look. "I know it's been hard on you having him back home. You two were so close for so long, and now you have Walker in your life and I just don't want there to be any problems today with them both being here, that's all I'm saying."

"You do know Walker and I are just friends, right, Mom?"

She gave me a knowing look, as if to say she wasn't buying that one bit. Then Peyton called her away. I groaned in frustration and went to check on the table to ensure all was set properly, just as Walker and Ben wandered into the dining room looking like old friends.

Someone had set out place cards and I immediately noticed that they had sat Walker next to me and Ben across from me. I frowned at them.

Walker took notice and shook his head. He snatched the card with his name on it and walked around until he found Ben's and switched them.

"They're going to notice," I assured him.

He shrugged. "So what? It's asking for trouble. At least this way if Ben's wolf starts to act up, you're within arm's reach to calm him."

When it was finally time to sit down to eat, I saw a few questioning exchanges when Ben sat next to me, but no one came right out and said anything. We made it through dinner without a hitch.

Peyton hadn't said a word to me or Ben so far, but she kept sending glares my way. Ben caught one of them and I felt his wolf stir. I discreetly moved my hand onto his thigh and he instantly calmed. I bit back a grin knowing I had that kind of power over him.

When dessert was served without a single question or anyone even noticing there was something going on between Ben and me, I saw him grin and wink at the twins sitting across from us. They both scowled in frustration, having been certain they were going to win their bet.

As the boys cleared their dessert plates, all three of them asked to be excused. That's when Ruby started in on Walker and Ben. She basically began interrogating the two of them until Dad stepped in and told her it was enough.

I could feel Ben's agitation rising again and a few minutes later everyone started holding their noses and complaining. I glared at Ben.

"It wasn't me," he said.

Everyone turned to look at Walker.

"No way was that me. God, it stinks," he complained.

"You're the only two unmated males here," Ruby pointed out. "One of you is clearly trying to claim Shelby."

"What?" I shrieked. "I smell that stench, too. It's not for me. I mean if it was, aren't I supposed to like the smell?"

Ben looked at me in confusion and shrugged. "I swear it's not me."

That's when I heard the giggles from under the table. I pulled my chair back and lifted the tablecloth to find Oscar, Will, and Troy lying on the floor with some kind of aerosol can in their hands. Ben leaned down and snatched one of the cans from Will.

"Can O Fart? Really?"

Maddie glared at Liam. "Are you serious?"

"Oscar, that was not to be used at the dining room table. Now get off the floor and apologize to your grandparents for trying to ruin Thanksgiving," Liam scolded them.

"You two as well," Ben added.

The boys stood and apologized, but then Will smirked at Ben.

"You guys really thought it was a Ben, didn't you?" Will asked.

Ruby laughed. "No, we all thought it was Walker. Were you guys the ones that changed the place cards, too? Because we were trying to avoid something like this from actually happening."

"Why would you think it was Walker?" Oscar asked.

"Oh, sweetie, um, you see, Walker and Aunt Shelby are . . ." Peyton started.

"Friends," Walker finished. He looked right at Ben, trying to give him reassurance. "We're just friends."

Peyton's face fell and she turned on me. "You said he was definitely not your true mate."

I dropped my head, knowing my face was likely ten shades redder than usual.

"His wolf hadn't even come in before he left, Pey," I said weakly.

Lily burst out laughing. "Oh my God! Are you saying Ben really is your true mate?"

All eyes flew to us. I dared a quick look at Ben. He didn't seem put off one bit; instead he was grinning proudly and reached for my hand on top of the table to give it an encouraging squeeze.

Mouths dropped open in surprise and the entire room went quiet.

"Is this true?" Dad finally asked.

I sighed. "Yes," I finally managed to say.

Ben immediately began to relax. I somehow knew he was happy to have it out in the open.

"Look, we didn't know until he showed up in my classroom three days ago," I blurted out.

"You still didn't know then," Peyton pointed out.

"I sure did," Ben added. "No doubt about it."

"I know, Peyton. I'm dealing with it," I told her. I knew she was worried about me. She understood how massive this was, more so than anyone else.

"You always told us he was the one," Mom said, wiping tears from her eyes.

"I did?"

"Since you were like two," Lizzy said.

"There's no way I knew back then," I laughed.

"I don't know, you were pretty convincing," Clara chimed in.

"Are you leaving her again without a word?" Peyton accused.

"Peyton, that's enough," Dad scolded.

"If I had known back then, I'd never have left to begin with," Ben said. "I figure I've got nine years to make up for, but I will." There was a promise in his voice, and he gave my hand another squeeze.

"Well, this is certainly a surprise, but a happy one," Mom proclaimed. "Welcome to the family, Ben." She rose and walked over to hug him. "Feels like you always were, this just makes it official."

"Thanks, Cora," Ben said.

It dawned on me that Peyton was the only person surprised by the announcement. It was as if everyone else had somehow expected it and went back to life as usual. What if I had chosen not to accept him? I mean, I hadn't even decided for sure myself. There was still so much we needed to talk about. Ben might not even want me still when he found out the truth about me. I started to panic.

"Hey, Sport, what's going on?" Ben whispered.

"I need to get out of here," I told him, fearing I was going into a full-blown anxiety attack.

Maddie walked over and hugged me. "I know that look, let's get you out of here." Then she turned to Ben. "Oscar's really enjoying having your brothers here. Is it okay if they stick around to play a while longer?"

"Um, yeah, sure. That's fine," he said, a little confused and looked like he was starting to worry about me.

"Take her home. Trust me. I'll tell everyone you left," Maddie said. "Call me if you need me," she told me with one last hug.

Ben took my arm and walked me outside. I was starting to gulp for air. Walker had of course noticed our hasty exit and came to check on me.

"Shit!" he said, taking my other arm and assisting Ben with getting me into the car.

Ben was quiet and didn't even growl at Walker for touching me.

Once inside the car, he started it up and took off, reaching his hand over to place it on my thigh. "Breathe, Shelby. In and out slowly. Find a happy thought." He smiled over at me and kept talking in a soothing voice. "Remember our first kiss? I was so jealous when you told me you were going to kiss Grayson Ward. I always hated that punk."

"You did?"

"Well yeah, I mean he always had a thing for you. I think that was why it was so easy for me to believe him when he told me you were his true mate. I was an idiot."

"You weren't," I managed to say. "You didn't know and didn't have any reason not to believe him."

I was starting to calm down some. My pulse was slowing back to normal and I wasn't facing an impending blackout any longer. I hadn't had an anxiety attack in a long time.

"I deal with a lot of PTSD in my field, you know. Do you want to talk about it?" he asked.

I shook my head. "Absolutely not, but I think we have to."

"What happened to you, Shelbs?" he asked quietly, as if he knew it was something terrible. It had been, but not in the way he was probably thinking.

As we drove through Collier, I redirected him towards the cemetery. I told him to park and without another word I got out of the car and started to walk. My hands were shaking so badly, and I was fighting not to cry. This was the day I'd always prayed wouldn't come, because it was easier to be angry at Ben for not being here than it was to just face the truth.

I stopped in front of the tiny grave. It was simply marked "Annabelle Grace" with one date. Only one other person in this world knew why it was there.

Ben shook his head the moment he saw the name, recognizing it as the one I'd always told him I'd name my firstborn daughter.

"I've never told anyone about this," I said softly. "Only Doc knows."

Ben hugged me tightly as I started to cry.

"The letters you sent to me at boot camp said you had something important to tell me. I always assumed it was about Grayson, but I know now that wasn't it," he whispered, trying to process everything.

I nodded against his chest and sniffled. "I wanted to tell you, but I didn't think I should over a letter. I was planning to tell you at your graduation, but . . ."

"But I told you not to come."

"Yeah. I was a bit of an emotional wreck over that and more than a little pissed at you. I hid the entire pregnancy. I didn't know what to do. Peyton doesn't even know the truth, no one does. I was twenty-seven weeks along, but people just thought I had gained a little weight, upset about you leaving. I was driving and started having really bad cramps in my stomach. I didn't realize they were contractions, but I lost control of the car and hit a tree. When I came to, there was blood everywhere. So much blood," I said, trying to keep my composure to just get through it all. "Doc happened to be driving by and found me. He rushed me to the clinic. I had to tell him about the baby. He tried to save her, but she was so tiny. She never even made a noise. Stillborn, he had called it."

"Oh God, no," Ben said.

I brushed away more tears. "It gets worse," I confessed.

Ben shook his head like he didn't want me to continue, but I knew I had to. He had to know everything.

"We've always talked about having a houseful of kids, Ben, but that's not going to happen. I didn't just lose our daughter, but any chance of ever having kids again."

"What?" he asked, sounding like he was stuck in a haze. I understood that feeling far too well.

"There was so much blood. The accident caused a placental abruption and the damage was severe. Doc had to do an emergency hysterectomy just to save my life. I literally don't have the parts needed to bear you a child. I can't have any more children, Ben."

Ben

Chapter 14

My heart was breaking as I stood there staring at the tiny grave and listening to the story Shelby told. No wonder she had been so mad at me. No wonder she felt like she needed to protect herself from me. I had abandoned my mate when she had needed me the most. I couldn't even imagine her going through all of that alone.

The military had hardened me, and I couldn't remember the last time I had shed a tear, but I stood there holding her and started to cry. It was like the floodgates had opened up and I couldn't stop the trail of tears from falling. My heart ached for the child I never knew. It hurt for Shelby having to face it by herself. Why hadn't she leaned on her family? I knew she was tough, but this was beyond that. And I cried for the family we would never have.

As our combined sobs began to ebb, I sat down on the ground and pulled Shelby down with me. Without asking, I picked up a rock and channeled my wolf strength to carve into the headstone "Shay" beneath her name. She wasn't some unknown child, she was my daughter and I would claim her as such.

My action made Shelby sob a little longer, but she was smiling through her tears.

I wasn't sure how long Shelby and I sat there just holding each other, but when night began to fall, I knew I should get her home. We were both emotionally tapped out, and it would take me a while to fully process everything she'd told me.

The drive back to the Alpha house was a quiet one.

"Are you okay?" she asked as I parked the car.

"No, but I will be. I know that wasn't easy on you either. Are you okay?"

She nodded. "Yeah, I am. It was nice to share her with someone."

I walked her into the house. It was still quiet, a sign no one was home yet. She walked upstairs to her bedroom and I followed. I didn't know what to say or do.

"Since I'm cleaning my slate with you today, there's something else you should probably know."

I wasn't sure I could handle too much more in one day, but I didn't tell her that.

She let us into her room and closed the door behind her. She motioned for me to sit on the bed, and then went to her closet. A minute later she came out with a box and set it on the bed. Then she went back to retrieve another, and another.

"What's this?" I asked.

Shelby looked a little uncomfortable and I could feel her anxiety rising through our bond.

"Open them," she finally said.

I hesitated for a moment and then lifted the lid off the first box. Inside there were envelopes, hundreds of them. I pulled one out and saw it was addressed to me.

Shelby took a deep breath. "I never stopped writing to you, Ben. I just stopped mailing them."

I stared at the boxes in awe. "Every day?" I asked.

"Every single day until two months ago," she confirmed. "Peyton knew about it and thought I was crazy for it, but I kept writing. I guess it became more like a journal after a while, but they're all there."

I picked one out at random and opened the letter.

Dear Ben,

Annabelle would be turning two today if she were still with us. I have no idea how I'll ever face you again knowing I killed our daughter. . .

I sucked in a deep breath, unable to finish reading it. Of all the letters to pick, why did it have to be that one?

"You didn't kill her, Shelby!" I said.

"What?" she asked, grabbing the letter from my hands. She sighed. "You had to pick that one first? Of all these letters?"

Shelby wiped another tear form her cheek and started laughing. I didn't know why we were laughing, but I joined her.

I pulled her over to me and leaned down to kiss her. The mood changed instantly between us. Shelby sobered, gave me another quick kiss, and pulled back to stare into my eyes.

"You can't possibly want me after everything I told you," she said.

I didn't understand how she could conceivably think that.

"Sport, there's never been anyone else for me, ever. What happened was awful, and I hate that I wasn't here to go through it all with you, but I love you all the more for it."

"You love me?" she asked.

I scowled at her and brushed away a piece of hair sticking to her cheek.

"I've never stopped loving you, Shelby, and I never will."

She started to sob again, but I pulled her back into my arms and kissed the tears away. This time I couldn't restrain myself from stopping there. I broke away from her long enough to move the boxes off the bed.

Shelby was nervous, and if I was being honest, I was a little too as I fumbled to find the hem of her dress and pull it up over her head.

"I'm a little out of practice with this," I told her.

She giggled, "Me too."

As I discarded her bra, I stopped to admire the beautiful woman she'd transformed into.

"So perfect," I said as I kissed her again.

As she reached for me, I instantly grew hard. Relief washed over me and boosted my confidence. With sure hands I carefully removed the rest of her clothes and set about getting reacquainted with my mate.

"Mine," I told her, nipping at her breasts.

She giggled and threw her head back like she was breaking free of the past between us. Our slate was clean, and this was the beginning of a second chance for the both of us.

"I'm yours if you still want me," Shelby whispered.

I nuzzled into her soft belly. "I'll always want you, Sport. Always."

I think she expected me to seal our bond right there, but I knew her family could return at any moment. This wasn't the time for that, this was the time to explore and enjoy each other. In a weird way, this was the ultimate makeup sex.

My entire focus was on her and each orgasm I brought her to, first with my fingers, and then with my mouth, only heightened my need for her. I was buzzing with anticipation when I slowly slid into her.

Just like our first time, all those years ago, there was a sense of completion being so intimate with her. I felt whole again as I froze and just allowed it all to sink in until she started to wiggle beneath me unable to stand it any longer.

I kissed her breathless as we found our rhythm. We were so in sync with each other it was crazy, so much more than just sex. The buildup was intense, but the frenzy that consumed us both as we headed for the edge was insane. I had never felt so alive in my entire life as I crested with the strongest orgasm of my life.

I collapsed on top of her as my body still convulsed from the intensity of everything. Before my breathing started to regulate again, I rolled to my side, scared I'd crush her, and pulled her to me.

She kissed my chest. "I love you, Ben."

"I love you too, Sport," I said.

After the emotional rollercoaster and the greatest sex of my life, I was exhausted in mind and body. I closed my eyes and immediately drifted off to sleep.

When I awoke the sun was shining through the window and it took me a moment to get my bearings straight. It dawned on me that it was morning. I stretched and Shelby groaned and snuggled closer to me.

A smile crossed my face as I started remembering, and I thought of the boys.

"Shit!" I said, jumping out of bed and searching for my clothes.

Shelby moaned. "What's wrong?"

"The twins. Shelby, we fell asleep and I forgot about the boys!"

She laughed. "Relax. Maddie brought them back here. They're down the hall having a sleepover with Oscar. You were out pretty hard."

As she said the word "hard" she looked down at me and grinned as she licked her lips.

"Shelbs, everyone's home. My brothers are just down the hall," I tried to reason, knowing if she approached me, there was no way in hell I could say no to her. After last night, I'd be more than happy to never leave this bedroom ever again.

"I have a dampener," she teased.

I groaned, then dove back into bed as her laughter filled my head and brought more happiness than I knew possible. Maybe there was time for a quickie before we started the day.

Shelby

Chapter 15

When I walked down to the kitchen, I knew everyone would know. The thing was, I didn't care.

"Oh my gosh, you sealed it," Maddie said when I walked in.

I shook my head. "No, we didn't."

"Girl, with the way you're glowing now, that must have been some amazing s-e-x," Lily said, making me blush all over.

"Why didn't he seal the deal?" Thomas asked.

"Sorry, not something I'm discussing with my baby brother. Way to gross me out," I complained.

"Like he's one to talk. They've known for three days, Thomas. How many did it take you?" Lily teased.

"You're feeling all kinds of sassy today, slugger. Keep it up and I'm going to have to take you home and put you in your place," he said, pulling Lily into his arms and kissing her.

She threw her head back and laughed. "Was that supposed to be a threat or a promise?"

He shook his head, smacked her on the butt, and left the room.

"Hmmm, having mating males around always makes him a little wild. Do me a favor and let those hormones fly a little longer, Shelbs. Hold off on sealing your bond a few more days at least."

Maddie and I both looked at each other. "Ew!"

"Unless you want to hear stories about Liam, I suggest you keep that shit to yourself, Lil," Maddie threatened.

We were all laughing when Ben walked in. He stopped at the doorway and started to turn and walk back out.

I walked over and wrapped my arms around his waist letting him know we were okay, more than okay, really.

"Coffee's hot and ready, much like your mate," Lily said.

I blushed and shot her a look.

"Just how I like both," he mumbled with a grin as I smacked him on the chest. He leaned down to kiss me before moving over to fix his coffee.

There was such a weight lifted from my shoulders after sharing Annabelle with her father. It was so surreal, and despite it all, he was still here. I didn't understand why, but I wasn't going to look a gift horse in the mouth.

Mom walked in and startled. "Ben, I didn't realize you were having a sleepover, too," she said slyly, waggling her eyebrows up and down behind his back as Lily and Maddie hooted.

"Sorry, Cora. I'll try not to make a habit of it," Ben said sheepishly.

"Make a habit of what?" Dad asked as he walked into the kitchen, too.

"Sleeping over," Mom informed him.

"Oh." Dad shrugged. "You're always welcome here, Ben. This is Shelby's home, too." Dad put his arm around my shoulders and gave me a squeeze.

"This is getting way too weird," I grumbled.

"Thanks for watching after the boys last night, Maddie," Ben said.

"It was no problem. Shelby called to arrange everything, and the boys were ecstatic," she said.

Ben gave me a weird look. "You did that?"

I shrugged. Ben had been emotionally and physically drained when he crashed. Not that I blamed him one bit. I had dropped a Hiroshima-sized bomb on him last night. Taking care of the twins was the least I could do.

"What time are you hitting the road?" I asked him.

Ben looked at his watch. "Probably should have already left," he admitted. "How much time do you need to get ready?"

I blinked in surprise. “Um, not long,” I said.

I knew he was taking the twins to visit with their parents. The doctors Thomas had lined up for them wanted to keep Marnie in the hospital, too, at least for post-surgery observations. They were the same team that had helped Lizzy and Cole after a terrible accident that had nearly cost them both their lives. I knew they were human, but they also knew all about shifters and the unique concerns with fully mated pairs. I had been told not to question it.

“Where are you headed?” Dad asked.

“To the hospital to visit Mom and Dad. I got a couple texts yesterday saying the surgery went well,” Ben said.

“Oh, that’s wonderful news. Send them both our love,” Mom said.

“I will, thanks,” he told her.

“I’ll get the boys moving,” Maddie offered.

“Before MC leaves, I’m taking your girl hostage. With this new revelation, we desperately need a ladies’ night,” Lily told Ben.

He laughed. “Understood.”

As Ben and I headed back upstairs I was struck by just how surreal the morning had been.

“Everyone’s handling the news really well. It’s weird,” I said.

“You and I have been together practically our entire lives. I don’t think anyone is all that surprised to see us together now.”

“Maybe.”

Once in my bedroom, I shut the door behind us. Ben turned and pinned me up against it. I sighed as his lips descended on mine.

“I’m going to have a terrible time trying to keep my hands to myself today,” he admitted.

“I have a feeling your mother isn’t going to be as happy about our news as my family seems to be,” I said. I was more than a little nervous to tell her.

“Why would you think that?”

I shrugged.

“Sport?”

“Fine, she was warning me off yesterday, reminding me that you broke my heart last time you left and that you were only home for a few weeks and would be leaving me again.”

He growled and punched the door above my head as he pushed away from me. “That’s what the two of you were talking about?”

I nodded. I wasn’t scared by his action, I could literally feel his frustration.

“It’s not going to be like that this time, Shelby. You are my mate. As long as it doesn’t put the team in jeopardy, we can video chat every day. Yes, I have to go back, but it will only be temporary. I don’t want to leave you, but I’m going to have to. You know that, right?” he said, running a hand across his short-cropped hair.

“I know,” I told him. “And I trust you when you say this time will be different.” I prayed he was right, because I didn’t think I’d survive it if he went dark on me again, this time with an unresolved bond.

“You look worried,” he said with a frown.

“Can’t help it, but I’m hoping for the best,” I said honestly.

Ben sighed and pulled me back into his arms. “I know I have a lot to prove to you this time. Just hang in there, Sport. I’m not going to let you down.”

“Did you know that Lizzy and Cole went a decade with an unresolved bond? I’ve seen what that does to a person, Ben, and it terrifies me.”

He kissed the top on my head. “I’m not leaving here with anything unresolved, Shelbs. That’s a promise.”

I stared up at him, surprised by what he’d just said.

“You want to seal the bond?” I asked.

He chuckled and brushed the hair from in front of my eyes. “Is that really so shocking? It took a lot of restraint not to do it last night.”

“Why didn’t you?” I asked.

“Last night was about you and me, Sport. It’s been too long. I’ve missed you so much and I didn’t want to get caught up in the frenzy of the bond. I just wanted you,” he said honestly.

“Last night was perfect.”

I rubbed myself against him, feeling how much he still wanted me. He checked his watch and I knew he was seeing if we had enough time for a quickie. The knock on the door told us both we did not.

Ben groaned in frustration. “Go get ready,” he finally said.

"You sure? I could take care of that pretty quickly," I said, patting the front of his pants.

"That is not helping one little bit. Are you taking a shower?" he asked.

I shrugged. "Probably should, but not sure I have enough time. I'll just brush my hair and throw it up in a ponytail."

"Good, because I need a quick cold shower before we go," he said.

I laughed and patted him on last time. "Offer still stands."

Another knock at the door had him growling as he headed for the bathroom.

I quickly changed clothes and grabbed the brush before opening the door.

"Is Ben ready?" Troy asked.

"No, he just jumped into the shower. He'll be a few more minutes."

"It's like a five-hour drive. We need to hit the road," Will whined.

"Did you guys get breakfast yet?" They both shook their heads. "Head on down to the kitchen. Mom should be there and will round something up for you. If not, just help yourselves. I'll speed up Ben."

"Are you coming with us, Ms. Shelby?" Will asked.

I smiled. "It's okay to just call me Shelby outside of school. And yes, is that okay with you guys?"

They shared a look and shook their heads.

"I'm still worried you're going to get hurt when he leaves," Troy admitted. "I don't want you to be hurt, Shelby."

I hugged them both. "It's a risk I'm willing to take, Troy. It will suck for all of us when he has to return to his unit, but that doesn't mean we should push him away. We need to treasure the time we do have with him, okay?"

Troy nodded and I shooed them back downstairs.

When I turned around, Ben was standing there in just a towel watching me. There was love shining in his eyes.

"Thank you. I think Troy really needed to hear that," he said softly.

"We have a long drive ahead, so get dressed," I told him, not wanting to discuss it any further.

When we finally got back downstairs, ready to go, Walker was waiting for us. He smiled and hugged me, ignoring Ben's warning growl as he passed by to get the twins.

"Thomas made arrangements himself. I'm driving," he said.

"The whole five hours?" I asked skeptically.

Walker laughed. "No, just to the airfield. The Collier plane is gassed and ready. There will be a car waiting when you arrive to take you to the hospital."

"Is he still in his office?" I asked, wanting to thank my brother.

"Nah, some important meeting on the green."

I rolled my eyes, knowing how much my brother loved playing golf. It had become one of his new obsessions in life. I would never understand it.

Ben rounded up the boys and we headed outside. They all went straight for my car, but Walker whistled and redirected them to an SUV.

"What's going on?" Ben asked.

"Change in plans," I told him.

He scowled. "We really need to hit the road. We should have left hours ago."

"It's okay. We're flying instead," I said.

"We are?" Will asked.

I nodded.

"Cool!" Troy approved.

"We've never been in a plane before," Will admitted.

I wasn't surprised to hear it. Most of our wolves never left Collier except to maybe drive into the surrounding towns when they needed something Collier couldn't provide.

"Are you sure about this?" Ben asked.

"Yeah, it's fine. Thomas arranged it. We're using the Pack plane."

When we arrived at the airfield, the boys nearly tripped over each other racing up the stairs to check the plane out. It wasn't big but it was functional. The inside featured plush seating for twelve. It also had a galley and two bathrooms. There was more than enough room for the four of us.

The pilot came out to greet us and apologized that he hadn't been able to line up a stewardess for the day on such short notice.

"It's fine," I assured him. "I know my way around the galley if we need anything, and besides, it's what, about a forty-minute flight?"

"Yes, ma'am. We'll be there before you know it."

"Cool!" the twins said in unison.

The captain took them up front and showed them the cockpit while he ran his pre-flight checks.

Ben and I took the seats at the back and buckled up. When they boys joined us, they chose the front row, as far away from us as possible.

Ben held my hand on takeoff but relaxed once we were in the air.

"Not a fan of flying?" I asked.

He shrugged. "I'm used to it but doesn't mean I have to like it. It's fine once we're actually in the air."

"Gage hates to fly and he and Clara travel everywhere for work. Whenever they have the time, he makes her rent a car, even if it means a few days on the road to get home. He's always saying that no shifter should ever be stuck in a tin can in the sky like that."

We both laughed.

"That's about how I feel, only with less options."

The flight was uneventful, as was the car ride to the hospital. I was quite nervous, unsure of how Marnie would take the news of me mating her son.

"Are you okay?" Ben asked me as we were walking in. He shooed the boys ahead of us and they quickly found their parents' room.

"I'm fine, just nervous."

"What on Earth do you have to be nervous about?"

I cut my eyes at him. "Really?"

"Sport, it's going to be fine," he tried to assure me.

Taking a deep breath, I started heading for the room where we'd watched the boys enter. Ben caught up next to me and wrapped a possessive arm around my shoulders. He kissed my temple before we walked in.

Both of his parents were sharing a bed and sitting up, listening to the boys talking animatedly. Marnie was the first to notice our arrival. She immediately took in the sight and her eyes started to tear up.

"What's the matter?" Don asked.

He followed her line of sight to the two of us.

"Benjamin!" he beamed, genuinely happy to see his son.

"Hey, Dad. You're looking good," Ben observed.

He hurried to his bedside to hug his father. I held back and gave them a minute to catch up feeling a little like I was intruding on their family moment.

Don finally looked up and smiled, motioning me to join them.

"Little Shelby Collier," he said affectionately. "It's been a long time since we saw the two of you together."

I leaned down and gave him a quick hug.

"Too long," Ben agreed, putting his arm around my waist and pulling me close to his side once again..

"They're true mates," Troy said as if it were common knowledge.

"What?" Marnie asked.

Ben beamed and squeezed me tighter as I shrugged.

"You don't have to worry about me, Marnie. I really don't think I'm getting rid of him so easily this time," I joked.

Ben

Chapter 16

I abandoned Shelby to walk around and hug Dad. He looked better than I expected.

"I hear the surgery went well," I said.

"It did indeed. They had to put steel rods to rebuild my leg. The good news is I will walk again, at least in human form."

"I'm so sorry, Dad," I said. It broke my heart to know he would never shift again.

"It's okay, son. I know it won't be easy, but I'm going to be okay. We all are. Ultimately your mother left the decision up to me and I decided that at least for now I would rather be whole in one form than crippled in both. And if I change my mind, Doc says he'll consider a scheduled amputation, so that's not entirely off the table, but for now, I think we're going to be okay."

"How about you, Marnie? How are you holding up through all of this?" Shelby asked Mom.

She reached for my mate's hand and squeezed it. "I'm okay. The pain is tolerable and they're letting us room together, which helps keep the wolves at bay. I'm afraid we're going to be here a couple more weeks, though."

"But Ben's going back in ten days," Troy said.

I didn't want to make promises I couldn't keep. I'd been granted two weeks of leave. I could request more, but there was no guarantee.

"It's going to be okay, guys," Shelby said. "You aren't getting out of your schoolwork that easily." Will groaned. "I'll make arrangements for them to stay at the Alpha house for as long as you need."

"Shelby, it's okay. We'll figure something out," Marnie said.

"It's not a problem, really. I'm sort of part of this family too now, right? If Ben can't be here, well, I am."

I smiled at her gratefully and nodded.

"She's right, Mom. I know how proud you both are, but Shelby's part of this family now. We may not have sealed our bond yet, but it's going to happen before I leave. She works at the school so keeping them on their schedule will be easy for her."

"Plus, there is plenty of room at the Alpha house. My parents and I are the only ones still living there. There used to be nine of us," she reminded them.

"I'll talk to Cora just to make sure it's no problem," Mom said.

"Mom, if it's a problem, Shelby can just stay at the house with the boys. We've got this. I don't want you and Dad worrying."

"We'll be fine, Mama. Shelby will take good care of us," Will confirmed.

"Yeah, that's cool with me, too," Troy said. looking relieved that we had a plan in place.

My parents were very proud and humble people, so I know it took a lot for Mom to reach for Shelby's hand and thank her, essentially accepting her offer to take care of my siblings.

We visited for a few more hours. There were lots of laughs and joy, but I could see as the day went by how exhausted my parents were. The boys didn't want to leave them, but I insisted. We had originally only planned to spend the day, most of which would have been driving, but since Thomas made alternative plans, they now included putting us up in a local hotel for the night so we would get two days with my parents. The plane was to fly us home the next night.

When we got to the hotel, I found Thomas was full of surprises. He had gotten us a penthouse two-bedroom suite. The boys' room had two queen beds, and then ours had a king. I owed Thomas big time and wasn't sure how I could possibly repay him.

Shelby didn't seem to think anything of it. Rarely in our lives did moments arise that truly showcased our Pack status differences. This was one of those times, or maybe it was just me now. The army life was definitely not penthouse suites

"We didn't pack to stay the night," Troy said.

"I know, just get some sleep. Mom and Dad aren't going to care that we're in the same clothes as yesterday," I assured him.

"I'll be right back," Shelby said seconds before leaving the room. I didn't know what she was doing, but I couldn't just leave the boys alone to go after her. It set my wolf on edge having our mate out of sight in a strange place and I wondered, not for the first time, just how I was going to make myself leave her when the time came.

"I'm hungry," Will said.

Earlier, we'd had lunch at the hospital with our parents, but it was getting late in the evening and I had to admit that I was a hungry, too.

"Let's wait until Shelby returns and we'll discuss dinner then," I told them.

They retreated to their room and turned the television on. When I peeked in on them a few minutes later they were both buried in their phones.

Shelby didn't return until a full hour later and I had practically worn a trail in the carpet pacing the room waiting. When she walked in, she was loaded down with bags and boxes of pizza.

"Sorry," she said. "I figured everyone was getting hungry, but the pizza place took forever.

"Did someone say pizza?" Will asked as he poked his head back into the room.

"Wash up and let's eat," she said, smiling happily. "I'm starving."

"Me too," Troy agreed.

I took the pizzas from her and set them down on the dining room table. What kind of hotel room had a dining room?

"Where were you?" I finally asked. I needed to pull her into my arms to calm my wolf and ensure for myself she was okay. Actually, what I really needed was to drag her ass back to the bedroom and make her fully mine, but I did neither.

"I just grabbed a couple of things I thought we'd need. Thomas called and said that the plane was scheduled to pick up tomorrow evening, but if we needed more time to just let him know and he'd handle the arrangements."

"Give me your phone," I said a little more harshly than I meant to. She dropped the bags she was carrying to the floor and pulled it out of her back pocket to hand it to me.

I quickly programmed in my number, and then texted myself so I would finally have hers.

Shelby giggled as she watched, and that sound alone began to settle me.

"Why didn't we do that sooner?" she asked as she started sorting through the bags.

"What did you buy?" I asked.

"Not much, toothbrushes and toothpaste, some deodorant, because trust me, I work with these boys and it is not an age you want them ever going without it."

In spite of everything, I couldn't help but laugh at that. "What else?"

"A clean shirt for each of us and maybe a little something special for you later tonight if you behave."

That definitely caught my attention.

"Let me see," I said.

"No. I said, if you behave."

I started to stalk towards her, and she grabbed the bag that clearly didn't come from the same store as the others and hugged it to her chest. She rounded the table to the left, and I moved in to trap her. She faked and shot off in the other direction. She was fast, I had to give her that, but my wolf was gleefully on the hunt now.

In another surprise move, Shelby headed for the bedroom, but she couldn't get the door shut and locked before I was through it. She jumped onto the bed, still laughing and clutching the bag.

I sucked in a breath and wished we were alone.

"You are definitely not on good behavior," she said, but her cheeks were pink and her eyes full of mischief. She was enjoying the chase as much as I was.

Setting the bag down next to her, I channeled my wolf speed and snatched it from her.

"Cheater, you can't use your wolf powers."

It was my turn to laugh. "Sport, in my line of work, you learn quickly to commune as one with your wolf. We're pretty in sync and I don't even have to think about it anymore to channel his powers."

"That's pretty cool. Maybe you can teach me someday."

"Maybe," I started saying as I looked down into the bag and gulped at the sight of black, lacy lingerie with a pack of dirty dice on top. I pulled at the dice and read some of the categories. I quickly looked around to make sure my brothers weren't nearby and threw them back in the bag. "Shelby, Will and Troy will be right across the hall," I reminded her.

She shrugged and grinned. "Maddie called. Apparently Lily had her pack a few things for us." She opened her purse and pulled out a dampener and a box of condoms. "Don't need these," she said, tossing the condoms back into her bag. "But this, I will kiss her for when we get back." She grinned evilly back at me and I grew instantly hard.

It was difficult to remember just why I thought something was physically wrong with me in that department. With Shelby around, there was certainly no more concerns. I wasn't sure I'd ever be able to satiate my appetite for this woman.

"Can we go ahead and eat? I'm starving!" Will whined.

"We're coming," Shelby said.

"Bad choice of words," I mumbled under my breath.

Shelby threw her head back and laughed as she walked out of the room.

I took a deep, calming breath and readjusted my pants to make it less noticeable just how turned on I was and followed her out.

Dinner was actually nice. The boys were more relaxed and didn't seem as stressed after the day with Mom and Dad. They opened up a little about their concerns and thanked Shelby for being willing to keep them after I left. I tried to push down the guilt I felt. I didn't want to leave any of them, but I knew that each day that time got closer.

"Everything's going to be okay, guys. We're a pack, and the pack takes care of their own," she said.

"Thomas has gone above and beyond this time, though," Troy pointed out. "I mean, he's arranged everything for Mom and Dad and the Pack's paying for all their care, so we don't have to worry about medical bills. That's enough, but this place? This is above and beyond."

Will chimed in next. "Yeah, we would have just driven the five hours and probably just gone back home tonight or stayed in a motel somewhere along the way. I didn't even know places like this actually existed. You know, just in the movies. And a private jet? That was insane."

Shelby frowned. "That's the Pack's jet, you guys. Most people just don't realize they could ask for it."

Troy shot her a look like she was crazy. "That plane goes by Pack status, Shelby. You only say that because you're an actual Collier."

She frowned like she was contemplating what they were saying.

"Maybe," she said noncommittally.

I knew they were making her feel uncomfortable, so I changed the subject.

"Shelby picked up some new shirts and toiletries for each of us. Use them."

Will laughed. "Let me guess, deodorant?"

I raised an eyebrow up towards Shelby.

"Ms. Shelby goes on a weekly rant about the importance of everyone wearing deodorant. Most of us don't like it because of the smells and our heightened senses are starting to increase with puberty," Troy added. His voice cracked on the word puberty and caused me to fight back a smile. I didn't want to embarrass him, especially in front of Shelby, who they both clearly idolized.

"There is such a thing as unscented deodorant," Shelby said as both boys mouthed her words precisely, like they'd heard them a million times.

"She actually keeps stock in the little trial sizes and if someone comes into the room stinking, instead of calling that person out, she passes it out to every one of us and makes us put it on right there in class," Will informed me.

I couldn't help but laugh at that. "She's always been overly sensitive to smells, so I'm not surprised to hear that."

"You must know a lot about her, huh?" Will asked.

"There's very little I don't know about my mate," I said possessively, making her blush. I reached across the table and took Shelby's hand. "Go ahead, what do you want to know?"

"How old were you when you met?" Troy asked.

I smiled. "Two, I believe? Maybe even younger. Let's put it this way, the first picture of the two of us together shows us still in diapers."

"When did you first kiss?" Will asked, jumping to harder questions.

"Eighth grade," Shelby answered for me.

"Grayson Ward was her boyfriend at the time, and I got really jealous when she told me she was nervous about getting her first kiss at a party that weekend."

"So you what? Just planted one on her?" Will asked.

Shelby grinned at the memory. "He told me there was no way he was going to let Grayson ruin my first kiss."

I squeezed her hand and smiled.

"Dude, you had game!" Will said appreciatively. "You know he was lying and really just wanted to kiss you, right?"

She laughed. "I didn't know it at the time, but yeah, in hindsight, I knew."

"Caroline and I do everything together, but I can't imagine kissing her. She's my best friend. I just don't see her like that," Will confessed.

I shrugged. "That's where you and I differ, because I don't think I ever saw Shelby as anything but mine."

"Then why did you take off for the army and leave her behind?" Troy asked. "You broke her heart. I remember watching her cry, a lot."

Guilt was a strong emotion. I looked over at Shelby, thinking of everything she had to go through because of that one rash decision I made.

"It's okay," she tried to tell me, but I wasn't sure it was, and I didn't know how to stop feeling guilty about it, especially knowing I'd left not just her, but our daughter, too.

"I was wrong," I said. "I didn't know it at the time. I was told she had mated another guy, and I didn't know how to stay and live in a world where she wasn't mine. I didn't even give her the chance to explain it, I just tried to move on, to survive."

"Someone actually told you they bonded with Shelby?" Troy asked, sounding horrified.

I nodded, "Yup, and I was the idiot who believed him."

"What a douche!" Will said.

"Yeah, I was," I admitted.

Before Shelby could protest, Will spoke up. "Not you, Ben, the douche that would make up something so serious like that."

"Grayson Ward," Shelby sighed.

"He always seems so nice," Troy said. "I can't even imagine him acting like that."

"He definitely grew up a little after that, but he didn't really change until after he found his real true mate," she said. I hated hearing her defend him even that much. It had taken a lot not to hunt him down and rip his throat out for what he had done.

"What is it you do in the army anyway, Ben? And isn't that hard? Do you ever get to shift?" Troy asked.

"I couldn't imagine being stuck around all those humans all the time," Will added with a shiver.

"It's actually not so bad. I was picked up for an elite Rangers team pretty early on and I've been working with mostly the same guys my entire career."

"But they don't know about you, right?" Troy asked.

"Actually, they do. My entire unit is made up of shifters." I spent the next hour telling them a little about the guys I worked with and making them laugh with some of the crazy things we'd done.

When we hit a break in my stories, Will announced he was getting tired and going to take a shower and head to bed. He accepted the bag Shelby handed him and even leaned down to hug her before moving to hug me, too.

"I'm glad you're home, Ben, even if it's only for a few weeks. You're much cooler in person than over video chat," he said.

"I won't be gone so long next time. I promise you guys that," I said, making sure all three of them understood I meant it.

Troy followed Will back to their room as Shelby started cleaning up from our dinner.

"I think I could use a shower, too," I told her. The evening had been fun but surreal, a reminder of everything I'd been missing in my life.

I gave her a quick kiss and headed for our bedroom, deep in my own thoughts. I had a lot of decisions I needed to make about my future, and I needed Shelby to be a part of those discussions. This wasn't just my life anymore, it was ours.

I walked into the bathroom and stripped out of my clothes. I turned on the shower and entered. In the field we didn't always know how long we'd have running water, so you never wasted a drop waiting on it to warm up.

The icy water hit me hard as it tensed my muscles, but when the hot water kicked in, all that tension began melting away.

I was deep in thought when the curtain began to rustle. Shelby stepped in behind me. I turned to look at her gloriously naked body. Everything within me surged to claim her, but I resisted.

The mating call heightened my awareness of her, but the levels of protective and possessive needs I felt towards her were only minimally increased, because I'd always felt that way about this beautiful woman.

Aggressively I pulled her into my arms and kissed her. She moaned and sighed against me. My tongue swept in to duel with hers in a dance as old as time.

I pulled back to stare down at her. "I love you, Shelby," I said, and I planned to remind her of that every single day for the rest of our lives.

Shelby

Chapter 17

"I love you, too," I told him with a smile.

I had waited a lifetime to be with Ben, and now he was all mine. All the heartache and pain I had faced paled next to the happiness and joy he brought to my life. I trusted him when he said we were in this together this time. I didn't know what the future held for us, but I was excited to find out.

I wrapped my arms around his neck and pulled him down for another toe-curling kiss. God, Ben could kiss.

He had always been handsome and confident. As a teen I had thought he was muscular and strong, but how very wrong I had been. The years in the army had done his body good. He was chiseled and hard, yet he melted against me with a softness he shouldn't possess. He was once again careful to take care of my needs first, as I breathlessly withered in his solid arms.

I tried to reach for him, but he stopped me with a growl.

"I'm not done with you yet," he said, making my body quiver with anticipation. "And if you touch me right now, this night is going to end much too quickly." There was so much promise in his voice. I doubted I could ever tire of the thrill I felt being with Ben.

He carefully washed up, and then started on me, even taking the time to massage my scalp as he washed and rinsed my hair. Every nerve in my body was on fire by the time he turned off the water and dried us off.

I yelped in surprise when he lifted me easily into his arms and carried me to bed. He was so gentle when he laid me down, letting my legs hang over the side at my knees. He dropped to the floor and gently nudged them apart as he stared up at me with an evil grin.

I obeyed and closed my eyes, allowing myself to simply feel. The brush of his day-old beard against my thighs made me wiggle, but he pinned me down and diligently set about to pleasure me until I was seeing stars dancing behind my eyelids.

Satisfied, he began kissing a path up my body leaving goosebumps along the way. I opened my eyes to see the cocky smirk on his face. I knew he was proud of the fact that he'd made me melt into a puddle of goo.

With a strength I didn't know I possessed, I pushed him to the side, so that he landed with a thump on the bed next to me, and I forced my Jell-O like legs to move across the room. I retrieved the bag of my earlier purchases and blew him a kiss as I disappeared into the bathroom.

Looking in the mirror, I barely recognized my flushed complexion, wide eyes, and swollen lips. I pulled out the lingerie I'd bought and shimmied into it. I felt sexier than I ever had before. I chose to leave the matching panties in the bag. They were too pretty to risk being destroyed in a moment of passion.

I stood in the doorway of the bathroom leaning up against the frame as I waited for him to see me. His head slowly turned, and his breath hitched as his eyes drank in the sight of me. It gave me confidence as I slowly walked over to the bed and climbed up to straddle him.

He immediately reached for me, but I deflected his advances easily. I had already had two massive orgasms and needed a little break to recover. Besides, it was my turn for a bit of foreplay.

"No hands," I warned him, holding his arms above his head as I lowered myself down to kiss him.

I didn't know how a simple kiss could already begin to turn me on once more; then again, there was no such thing as simple where Ben was concerned.

I left his lips and kissed a path along his jaw, down his neck, stopping with an evil smirk to nibble on the place I planned to someday mark him. He growled and abandoned my no-touching policy quickly.

I sat back up and shook my head. He closed his eyes and groaned but obeyed once again as he bent his arms behind his head. I left his neck with one final kiss and continued my explorations of the various textures and planes of his body.

When I reached my final destination, one lick had him nearly jumping out of his skin and no longer able to keep his hands to himself. He threaded his fingers through my hair and stilled my actions.

"Shelby," he growled in warning.

I looked up and grinned at him. I loved seeing him so undone and on the verge of losing control. There was something so powerful in knowing I was his kryptonite.

Already hot and ready for him, I abandoned my mission and straddled him once again. His hands moved to my hips to help guide me in a show of control I knew he didn't feel. I threw my head back and welcomed the sensations of our joining as one, and then took what I needed quickly, knowing the state I had worked him up to already.

"Ben," I cried as I found my release.

He grabbed my hips and aggressively stilled my movements as they triggered his own orgasm. He was practically vibrating and had broken out into a sweat. Combined with the wild look in his eyes, it was the hottest thing I'd ever seen in my life.

I sat there staring down at him for what felt like an eternity before leaning down and kissing him. He repositioned us to spoon me from behind as we cuddled and talked late into the night about anything and nothing at all, both of us still avoiding any discussion of a future together.

The next morning when I awoke, I was still safely tucked in his arms. It was a surreal feeling and one I never wanted to let go of. He kissed my shoulder, letting me know he was awake as I rolled to face him.

"Good morning," he said. "I could really get used to this."

I grinned but knew he couldn't commit to that yet. If he could, he would have already claimed me. I wasn't sure what was holding him back. I kissed him, morning breath and all, just to distract me from that line of thinking.

There was a knock at the door. Ben wrapped the blanket tightly around me and ensured I was fully covered before he hit the dampener on the nightstand and told them to come in.

It was a little awkward as the twins walked in as I lay there with nothing but a tiny negligee covering me under the thick blanket.

"Sorry. We didn't want to bother you, but there's someone here looking for you, Ben," Troy said.

"Trust me, we did not want to disturb you," Will said dramatically.

I laughed. "It's okay. Who is it?"

Troy shrugged.

"A Patrick O'Connell?" Will said.

"Patrick's here? Why?" I asked looking to Ben.

He shrugged, looking like an older version of Troy.

"I only know the name because Walker mentioned it," he said.

"Close the door, and tell him we'll be right out," I told the boys.

As soon as the door was shut, I jumped out of bed and went to the bags to throw on some clothes while Ben dressed, too.

"What were you and Walker talking about Patrick for?" I asked.

"He said this guy was overseeing Westin Force for Kyle and rumor had it they might have an opening on their Bravo team. I was going to put in some calls next week just to feel out my options," he said.

I didn't know much about Westin Force, though I'd seen a few instances of the kind of things they did. I wasn't sure I wanted Ben to have any part of that. Then I remembered, that's probably what he does. He hadn't talked much about his actual job in the army, but as a member of an elite Rangers unit, I could imagine. Still, I couldn't bring myself to ask him.

Once we were both presentable, we walked out to greet him. Before I could register Patrick's presence, I was met with a squeal of excitement as his mate, Elise, threw her arms around me.

"Elise, what are you doing here? The boys said Patrick was here."

"Yeah, apparently he wanted to talk face-to-face with your new mate, so I tagged along when I heard you were here, too," Elise said.

I didn't know Elise all that well. She was a year older than me, so we had attended Alpha camp together, but weren't close friends like our sisters, Lily and Maddie, had been. Still, we had always been friendly, and I'd visited with her family enough times to get to know the adult Elise since Madelyn moved to San Marco.

"Ben, this is Elise and her mate, Patrick," I said, making the introductions.

"I hear you're just the man I need," Patrick told Ben.

"Depends on what you're offering, man. Walker and Cole only told me a little about the operation you're running over there, but enough that I'm interested in hearing more."

They jumped right into business, as Elise rolled her eyes and pulled out a box of doughnuts and some orange juice she'd brought for breakfast.

The boys showed up out of nowhere to grab a couple handfuls with quick thanks before retreating back into their own room.

"Cute kids," Elise commented.

"Yeah, they are. I have them both for English this year."

"That's right, Lily told me you were teaching now." Elise frowned as she looked over to Ben. "How attached are you to that job? If Ben takes Patrick's offer, you know it would mean a relocation to San Marco."

My heart dropped. Logically I knew that, and I was surprisingly okay with it. I was more disappointed that Ben hadn't actually mentioned it. Would he even want me to go with him? He called me his mate and made sure everyone else knew it too, but he hadn't actually claimed me or made any move to do so.

"I hadn't even thought of it," I told her honestly.

Ben reached over and linked our fingers together. "We're not making any decisions today. We need time to consider all our options and determine what's best for the both of us," he said.

I let out a sigh of relief and fought back tears. He had made little comments here and there, but it was the first real thing he'd said about a future together for us. I had been so certain that he would mark me as his last night, that my unfounded fears had surfaced after he didn't.

"Of course you guys don't want to make a rash decision like that," Elise said.

"Walker tells me you're in the army?" Patrick asked Ben.

"Yeah, Rangers."

"How much time do you have left on your contract?"

"A few months if I don't re-up," he said.

I knew Ben had said he could get out soon, but we hadn't discussed any of the details on that. I drank in everything the two of them said as I tried to picture myself in Ben's life permanently.

"Do you have a secure place we can talk, Ben?" Patrick asked.

He shrugged. "There's a dampener in the bedroom."

"Perfect. If you ladies will excuse us, I'm going to let you catch up while Ben and I talk."

I nodded, but I wasn't happy about being left out of the conversation.

Ben

Chapter 18

I closed the bedroom door behind me as Patrick took a seat on the little couch in the corner and I grabbed the desk chair and rolled it over to sit across from him.

"You haven't really talked about any of this with Shelby yet, have you?" he asked.

I shrugged. "A little. She knows I'm looking into my options."

Patrick shook his head. "Let me give you a little advice, don't exclude her while you try to figure it all out on your own. If she's your mate, Ben, the decisions you make going forward directly impact her, too. You're two parts of a whole. I can't have one of you and not the other. Which is why I prefer single guys if I'm being honest. I'm only here as a favor to the Collier family. If you were mating any other person, I would have passed you over quickly."

"With all due respect, Patrick, who I mate has no bearing on my ability to fill the position you're looking to hire," I said, feeling on edge and defensive.

"I noticed you haven't marked her yet. May I ask why?"

"Because with everything going on, we're both adjusting and I don't want to rush it and deal with the frenzy of bonding I've heard about while dealing with watching my brothers, and having my parents stuck in the hospital. It's not really any of your business, but

I assure you, Shelby is mine, marked or not. She always has been. I was just too stupid to realize it."

He nodded. "Elizabeth filled me in a little on your history with Shelby. Are you going to want some downtime with her, once you're out? Maybe start a family or something?"

I cringed and shut my eyes not wanting to face that reality.

"I hit a sore Sport. You'll learn quickly that I have no personal boundaries with my guys. I need to know everything and anything that could comprise a mission."

"Lucky for me, I'm not one of you guys," I reminded him.

"You don't want kids?" Patrick guessed.

I glared at him. "Of course I want kids, and a family with Shelby, but that's not in the cards for us," I growled, not meaning to let that information escape, but at the same time needing someone to know.

Patrick sighed and nodded. "Tell me," he said and there was something about this man that made me want to, so I did.

"I just recently found out that I'd gotten Shelby pregnant from prom night of our senior year. She hid her pregnancy, but then lost the baby in a car accident."

"I'm so sorry, man. I can't imagine how much that's tearing you up. But you guys still have a lifetime ahead of you. You can have other children," he said.

I shook my head sadly. "Actually we can't. Doc had to do an emergency hysterectomy to save Shelby's life, so you see, we literally can't have children."

"Shit! I'm so sorry. Is that why you haven't claimed her?"

"What? No!"

"Does she know that? Sorry, I feel like I'm overstepping even for me, but the look on your girl's face out there didn't look like someone confident in your future."

I thought about that seriously. I had been trying to handle things on my own. Hadn't I told her I would be here for her this time? *Why would she believe you after the way you left her the last time, idiot?* a little voice in the back of my head reminded me.

"Shit!" I sighed. "Would you be opposed to having the ladies join us for this conversation? The actual job talk, not this," I said.

He smiled and nodded. "Yeah, sure. I have no secrets from my mate. She'll likely feign boredom, but if we're going to seriously discuss you working with me, then you're going to have to open up about what you're really doing in the army. Are you okay with Shelby knowing that?"

I cringed, knowing I definitely hadn't shared those details with her, but I nodded.

"I think I have to," I told him honestly.

"Now that's the right fecking answer as a mate." Patrick grinned, and stood up to walk to the door. He opened it. "Ladies, would you mind joining us for this?"

"Ugh, do we have to?" Elise complained.

Patrick laughed and shot me a "I told you so" look.

"Please, love. I think it's important for Shelby to be in on these conversations."

"Fine, come on," I heard Elise say.

Shelby walked in and I could feel her anxiety through our bond. I felt like an ass. I needed to do much better about reminding her that she was truly stuck with me this time.

Patrick had Elise help him carry in another couch from the living room area. I took that moment to reassure Shelby.

"It's going to be okay," I told her. "I want you to know that no matter what, you have final veto power. I don't care how amazing this job may sound for me, if it's not right for you, I'm out."

"Really?" she asked.

I nodded. "And I'm sorry we haven't taken the time to really talk about the next step in our plans yet, but you know I'm not going anywhere this time, right?"

She sighed. "Actually you're going back to the army in just nine more days."

I brushed her hair back behind her ear. "Only to wait out my contract. It'll be mostly paperwork and boredom for a few weeks to a couple months, counting down the days until I'm home to you. The guys will give me hell for it, but I had already started training my replacement before I came home."

"You did?" she asked.

I shrugged. "Told you the major was struggling to find a way around my last injury."

Patrick and Elise set the couch down and I moved over to sit on it with Shelby, while they took the small one.

"What injury?" Patrick asked.

"Shot to the back. Nicked my spine. I'm fully healed, no concerns, but it's the paper trail and timing that sucks. I ended up being medevacked for surgery. They did have to go in and remove the bullet, so it's all documented. Can't just miraculously get up and walk after that, now can I? Been stuck in a damn wheelchair for the last few months. Finally got back to my unit on a loophole of PTSD and depression. Convinced the doctors it would be best if I were reunited to help deal with that stuff."

"Who's the major you're working with?" Patrick asked and I immediately clammed up.

"I won't put my men in jeopardy, Patrick. That's one thing you should know about me right now. Those are my brothers. No names."

"I can appreciate that level of loyalty," he said. "But you have to give me something."

"This is all classified, right?" I said.

He nodded. "Of course. That's the only way I operate."

I took a deep breath and reached over to squeeze Shelby's hand. I was taking a giant leap of faith in the hopes for a better future for us. There weren't but so many job opportunities for a sniper or even a sharpshooter.

"First, tell me what your research pulled up on me, because I know you've background checked me already or you wouldn't be here wasting your time."

Patrick grinned. "Very little actually. It's driving Archie crazy. He's head of intelligence for the Force. There's nothing he can't crack, but on paper you're a staff sergeant in the army with a clean record and not one notable quality. They have you ranked under the Ranger's program, though, which is an immediate red flag for us that there's a lot more to you than we see on paper. Walker got that impression too, tells me you're a sharpshooter."

"Sniper, actually," I said. I felt Shelby stiffen next to me, but I leaned over and kissed her temple to let her know it was going to be okay. "But I'm marksman certified on just about any weapon you could put in my hands."

"You willing to prove it?"

"Any time," I said honestly, with no level of cockiness in my voice.

"My Bravo team has an opening. I won't lie, the majority of missions they go on do not require a sniper, but Silas Granger is the team leader and has been hounding me for months to get him one anyway. The fact that you can handle yourself up close as well is certainly a benefit. He's a gorilla shifter, and a bit of a son-of-a-bitch. Does that concern you?"

"My current leader is a bear, I'll deal."

That seemed to shock him, and I got the impression Patrick O'Connell was not a man used to surprises.

"You're telling me that your team leader is also a shifter?"

I nodded. "My entire team is, well, except for Jake, but who would have ever guessed that kid was human?"

"The U.S. Army has an elite Rangers team of all shifters?" Elise asked.

I nodded. "I'm actually surprised you don't know that already. Walker said you were looking to recruit from the elite teams."

"Honestly thought I'd have to bring in humans for that, and I've been on the fence about it," Patrick said. "This opens all new doors. Silas was a Seal, but his unit was not comprised of shifters."

"Best of the best," I assured him. I took a deep breath. "You hear of the Ghosts?"

"No fecking way!" Patrick exclaimed.

"What's the Ghosts?" Shelby asked quietly.

"That's the unofficial name my unit goes by. We're often called in for cleanups, in and out, undetected."

"Like ghosts," she whispered.

"Exactly."

"You're fecking telling me that the Ghosts are an all-shifter unit?"

"Always has been as far as I know, or at least since World War II, from what the major says."

"This is brilliant! Archie's gonna shit himself when I tell him this."

"We said confidential," I reminded him. "I have to protect my guys, too."

"I can appreciate that, but you don't understand. This guy prides himself on knowing everything, and I do mean everything, where shifters are concerned, and he has no idea there's an elite shifter team in the Rangers."

I laughed. "Fair enough, but no details, and I'm not giving up our actual unit name. You want an in to recruit from the Ghosts, I'll help you, but no names and no questions."

"Deal," Patrick said a little too quickly.

"And if Shelby and I decide this is the right path for us, then I want a trial period with the team."

"Can't do that, Ben. You're either in or you're not. Besides, I haven't even offered you a job yet," Patrick reminded me.

"No, but you will," I said confidently. "I am going to insist on a trial period. I'm not signing our lives away blindly, ever again." I had done that once with the army and managed to lose nine years with Shelby. I wanted a feel of exactly what I was getting myself into before committing long term.

Patrick shook his head. "Sorry, but that's just not possible. We take pride in the secrecy of Westin Force. You would learn too much, even on a trial basis. I can't afford that. You'll have to decide if you want this or not. No hard feelings."

"That's bullshit, and you know it. An organization like you're alluding to has to know of the Verndari."

Patrick's eyes widened with interest and he scooted forward a little in his seat. I knew I had his attention now and wondered if they weren't the real threat that led to this paramilitary unit he had created.

"What do you know about the Verndari?" Patrick asked.

"A hell of a lot, including the fact that they've developed a successful memory serum that will erase certain memories. If you don't have access to that already, I'll make certain I have some appropriated before leaving the army. If the trial doesn't go well and I decide I'm out, I'll take it and everything I've learned will simply disappear."

"It's not safe. I can't ask you to do that."

"It's safe enough, especially their latest version. It wouldn't be the first time I've had to erase a mission," I told him.

"They're using that shit on soldiers?" he asked.

"Only when absolutely necessary," I assured him. "The current batch only erases short term memories. I can remember being there, just none of the details. If I were ever called to testify, there would be no way for me to give away anything top secret. It would be the same in this case. I'd remember trialing the team, but unable to remember any details about it or what we did during my time with you. So do we have a deal or not?"

"I want samples of that shit to test in our labs," Patrick said.

"That's an easy one," I assured him.

Shelby was clinging to my arm and I knew that after this she and I needed to sit down and have a serious talk about a lot of things, and then I was going to claim my mate and prepare for our new life together.

Shelby

Chapter 19

It was good to be back home. After Patrick and Elise left, we went to visit with Ben's parents some more. A plan was in place for the twins so that Marnie and Don could recover in peace without stressing about the boys. I really didn't mind pitching in. I knew with Ben leaving soon, it would help me feel connected to him while he was gone.

I knew we needed to have some serious discussions, but I didn't know how to even begin to approach that. And the possible outcome of those discussions still scared me.

The twins had asked Ben to take them bowling and I had declined the offer to tag along. They needed time with their brother, and I needed to clear my head.

As soon as they dropped me off at the house, I jumped into my car and headed for Peyton's. I knew she only had a few hours at most and might already be heading to work to prep her station for the night.

I pulled up and hopped out. I was a little nervous walking to the door. I knew Ben was not one of Peyton's most favorite people in the world, but she was the one I confided in the most. I knocked on the door and waited.

Peyton answered and smiled. She opened her arms and I walked into them, accepting the hug she offered.

"I called it!" Peyton yelled towards the back of the house. Suddenly I was surrounded by each of my sisters.

"What are you guys doing here?" I asked.

"We knew you were coming back from your little family trip with the Shays and would need to talk about it. Austin's covering my shift at the diner and we have food and alcohol waiting," Peyton said.

I was a little put off because I did not want to discuss Ben with every single one of my sisters, but I was also overwhelmed by the care and love they each showed.

I filled my plate full in the kitchen and joined them in the back playroom. The babies were playing nicely in the corner.

"Where's Oscar?" I asked, knowing he and the twins had become fast friends and not wanting him to overhear us.

"Ben picked him up about fifteen minutes before you arrived to go bowling with the boys. You just missed them," Maddie said.

I had taken a few extra minutes on my drive over to swing by the cemetery and visit Annabelle. I took a deep breath, realizing there were a lot of things I needed to clear the air of tonight.

"So, no mark. Guess I lost that bet," Lily pouted.

"No mark," I confirmed.

"What's he waiting for?" Peyton grumbled.

"I don't really know, to be honest," I said.

"But everything is okay with you guys, right?" Clara asked, sounding concerned.

"Everything's great really," I said.

"So what's the problem?" Lizzy asked.

I shrugged. "Why hasn't he claimed me already? He says he's planning to before he leaves, but why wait?"

"Girl, you two have been through a lot together. I'm sure he's going to seal the deal. Just be patient," Ruby said.

"Says the girl who barely knew her mate's name when he claimed her," I grumbled, making the others laugh.

"You guys have a lot of history, Shelbs. Have you even gotten over being angry at him for leaving?" Peyton pressed.

"Yes, I have," I said honestly. "We've settled on all that. I know why he left the way he did, and he knows why I got so incredibly angry that he abandoned me."

"Why was that exactly?" Lily asked.

I could feel all the color drain from my face.

"What is it?" Peyton demanded. "There's something you haven't told me?" She sounded a little hurt.

I took a deep breath. "Yeah, there's something I didn't tell you, something I haven't told anyone, except Ben. I'd like to tell you guys," I said, tears already forming in my eyes. I swiped them away. "You may want to get the tissues first," I warned.

The worried looks my sisters shared did not go unnoticed.

"I'm okay, really. It's just hard to talk about," I said.

"You don't have to," Peyton told me.

"I know, and I know just telling you isn't going to magically make the pain disappear, but it's a start I need to heal."

Maddie came and sat by my side. She took my hand in hers. "Whatever it is, we're here from you," she assured me.

I rested my head on her shoulder. "Thanks. Um, well, where to start? I guess I should confess I lost my virginity to Ben the night of our senior prom."

Ruby started to laugh. "Seriously? That's so cliché! I honestly thought you guys had been hooking up long before then."

"Not all the way," I admitted.

"I thought you guys were just friends," Lizzy blurted out.

"Oh please, Shelby and Ben? Were you ever just friends?" Ruby asked.

I shrugged. "Yeah, I guess. I don't know. In hindsight I always knew he was mine, but he was my best friend and that was a little awkward to navigate through the teen years," I confessed.

"He was her first kiss, too," Peyton blurted out.

I laughed. "I'm pretty sure he's been my first everything in life."

"We're getting sidetracked," Lily pointed out.

I took a deep breath and decided to just dive right in. "Right after Ben left for the army, I found out I was a pregnant."

"What?" Peyton asked, sitting up and looking very concerned.

"You're serious?" Ruby asked.

All eyes were on me now, as fresh tears started to fall, and I nodded. Maddie hugged me closer. "What happened to the baby?" she whispered.

"You had disappeared, Ben was gone, and Mom was flipping out. It was just me and Thomas at home at that point and I didn't want to add any more stress to the family, so I hid it. At first I didn't want to stress him out by telling him through a letter, but then he asked me not to come out for his graduation. I was so angry with him for it, but it really wasn't his fault, because until a few days ago, I hadn't told him anything about her."

"Her?" Lily asked. "Annabelle Grace? The little mystery baby in the cemetery?"

"How did you know? Why would you even guess that?" I asked, surprised.

Lily shrugged. "I have a thing for cemeteries. I walk through there all the time and have always wondered about her story."

I started to sob, and Lily got up and hugged me.

"I was in an accident and she died. There was nothing Doc could do to save her. He had her buried there anonymously," I said. "I almost died too," I continued. "There was so much blood and he had to perform an emergency hysterectomy to save my life."

"No," Peyton gasped as she started to cry, too. "Why didn't you ever tell me?"

I shrugged. "I was numb afterwards and threw myself into helping Mom through Maddie's loss instead."

"Does Ben know you can't have children?" Maddie asked.

I nodded and started to really cry. "He does, and we've always wanted a family. I fear that's what is holding him back from claiming me."

"No way," Ruby said. "That man loves you unconditionally."

"He's an asshole," Peyton said.

"He's not, and if that is the case, I won't blame him for it. I can't have a baby ever. I can't give him that picture-perfect life we've always dreamed of." It was a burden I'd carried alone for too long and it felt good to admit it, like a weight had been lifted from my chest.

"I don't now about you ladies, but I need a drink," Lily announced.

"Pour me something strong," I said, making the others laugh.

We talked, laughed, and cried some more throughout the evening. When Ben stopped by to drop Oscar off, we were all pretty wasted, and my sisters attacked.

"Ben, come on in and have a drink," Lily said. "Have a seat." She directed him to a chair in the middle of the room as all my sisters circled around him. He looked a little horrified, which only threw me into a fit of giggles.

"How long have you ladies been drinking?" he asked.

"How long since you picked up Oscar?" Maddie countered.

"Shit, no good can come of this," he murmured.

"It's okay," Peyton announced, only mildly slurring her words. "I don't entirely hate you anymore, unless you haven't claimed Shelby just because she can't give you babies."

I sobered up quickly, feeling Ben's hurt and anger strongly through our bond. He stared at me and I started crying.

"I think I should take my mate home and I'm calling all of yours to come to do the same. Party's over."

"Party pooper," Ruby yelled at him.

Ben didn't even give me an opportunity to refuse, he simply swooped in, picked me up, and carried me out of the house.

"Oscar, come on, I'm dropping you off at your grandparents'," Ben said.

"Mom never gets drunk," Oscar said. "Wait, where's my sister? She was here with them."

"Bran picked up the babies a few hours ago. Relax, they're safe and sound at Ruby's," I assured him.

The car was silent as Ben drove from Peyton's house to mine.

"Stay put," he told me as he got out and walked all three boys to the front door. I watched as he spoke to my mom for a few minutes and then Oscar and the twins disappeared into the house while Ben returned to the car.

"I'm sorry," I said. "Wait, no I'm not. I needed to talk about her. I needed to tell my sisters about their niece. It felt good to share her with them."

"What was that bullshit about me not claiming because we can't have children, Shelby. Do you honestly believe that?" he asked.

I started to cry again. I was a drunk mess. "I don't know. You tell me. I told you everything, it's out in the open. You've had multiple opportunities to claim me, and yet you still haven't. What am I supposed to think?"

Ben pulled up to his house and without a single word he got out and walked around to open my door and pull me out. He insisted on carrying me into the house despite my protests, and then deposited me on the couch in the living room.

He started pacing back and forth and I knew he was upset.

"I don't want to answer you without putting some thought into this for fear I'm going to say all the wrong things out of anger," he finally told me. "And the thing is, you're so drunk, you might not even remember this conversation tomorrow."

"I'm not that drunk," I protested.

He kneeled before me and took both of my hands in his. "Shelby, I love you more than anything. I always have. I can see you're having a hard time trusting that, but I'm not going anywhere."

"Actually you are; you're leaving me in just a few days," I reminded him.

He growled. "That's not the same. I have an obligation that I have to see through. I'm not renewing my contract, but I do have to go and fill out paperwork and finalize things so I can have an honorable discharge, that's all. You'll hear from me so often you'll probably be sick of me before I even get back home. I'm not leaving you, damn it!"

I stayed quiet and just stared at him. I wanted to believe him, but I was bracing myself for the worst and we both knew it.

"And it's not that I don't want to claim you, Sport. In my heart, you're already mine and no mark will change that. I haven't sealed our bond simply because of everything going on right now. My parents are in the hospital and I'm responsible for my brothers. I sure as hell wasn't going to claim you last night with them in the next room, dampener or not. And before that there was a houseful of people. I don't want to worry about possible disruptions or someone barging in on us. I want it to be perfect, for you," he said, and I knew he was being entirely honest. "I didn't mark you the first night because we'd just dealt with Annabelle and our emotions were already high. I didn't think it was fair to you, but it's not that I didn't want to."

"I can't give you the family you've always dreamed of, Ben. Do you know how much that tears me up inside?" I said honestly.

He hugged me close to him as I cried some more.

“All I need is you, Sport. If we’re meant to have a family, and that’s still what you really want, well there are other ways to have kids. I’m not worried about that. And if I’m not being clear enough, let me put it this way: I love you. You are already mine and I will mark you as such when we have a second to ourselves where you aren’t this heavily intoxicated.”

In spite of it all, I laughed through my tears.

“I plan to spend the rest of my life with you by my side. I don’t know what that life is going to look like, and I can’t promise it will always be easy, but I’m in for the long haul, Sport, if you’ll have me.”

I nodded and smiled, throwing my arms around his neck. “I love you so much it drives me crazy sometimes. I’ve always been yours and I always will be.”

Ben

Chapter 20

I had a bottle of water and some aspirin ready the second Shelby woke up. I knew she was going to have one hell of a hangover. I just hoped she remembered some of our conversation from the night before.

I hated knowing that she had been worried that I didn't want to bond with her.

I heard her groaning from the other room, and she was holding her head when she finally walked in. "What happened?" she asked.

"Good morning," I said, getting up to hand her the water and medicine. "Here, this will help."

"I don't ever remember having a hangover this bad," she grumbled.

"Well, I'm pretty certain you and your sisters attempted to drink the equivalent of all the contents at Collier Liquor Store," I teased.

She groaned some more, but I helped her to the couch after opening the bottle and passing it to her. She downed the aspirin and sat back in agony. I couldn't help but smile at how adorable she looked even in her misery.

"I'll make breakfast if you're up for it. I wasn't sure you would be, though."

She shook her head, then grunted from the pain that little movement caused.

I felt riddled with guilt, like somehow her getting drunk had all been my fault. "I'm sorry," I told her.

"For what?" she asked.

"I shouldn't have left you yesterday. I should have reassured you every second since I returned that I'm not going anywhere this time."

"No, you have nothing to be sorry about. Just some insecurities on my part," she said sadly.

"I hate that I gave you those insecurities, Sport." I really did, too. If I hadn't been such a teenage moron, she wouldn't have anything to be worried about, and likely we would have been bonded years ago.

"Hey, we can't erase the past," she said, pulling me down beside her and wrapping her arms around me.

Something stirred inside me and I looked down at her to smile, showing off my canines that seemed to always appear now when she was close.

Shelby lit up and moved to straddle me. She pulled her hair to one side and exposed the slender column of her neck to me.

"What are you waiting for?" she asked.

I growled and kissed the spot I wanted to mark her. Seconds before my teeth were about to sink into her, my phone rang. I wanted to ignore it, but I couldn't. With a frustrated sigh, Shelby leaned over and checked it.

"It's the Alpha house number," she said, recognizing it immediately. She slid to answer. "Hello?"

"Tell me the boys are there with you," I heard Maddie say.

I grabbed the phone from Shelby and put her on speaker. "They're not here. I dropped all three of them off at the house last night," I told her, my heart jumping into my throat. Where the hell could they have run off to?

"Calm down, I'm sure they're fine," Shelby told us both. "We'll head in that direction and check a few places out."

"Thanks, Shelby. This really isn't like Oscar to just leave without telling someone."

"I know, it's not like the twins either," she said.

"Guess the wait continues," I said as she pouted. "Let's go find my brothers."

We left and got into the car. I drove slowly while Shelby's head was out of the window yelling for the boys.

"Stop," Shelby yelled as we passed the cemetery.

She was out of the car and running up the hill before I could even get the car in park. I channeled my wolf speed and easily caught up to her. We found the boys pulling weeds from around Annabelle's headstone.

"It can't be, he would have told us," Will insisted.

"Hey guys, you have a lot of people worried and out looking for you," I said.

Troy turned and glared at me. "Do you want to explain this?" he asked, pointing at the little grave.

"Do you want to explain why you guys are out here and not back at the Alpha house where I left you?" I countered.

"We didn't mean to be so long," Oscar said. "We were playing truth or dare, and I dared them to walk through the cemetery at night. It was my fault."

"But then we stumbled across this. Why does it have 'Shay' carved into it like this?" Troy asked.

Shelby pulled out her phone and called Maddie. "We found them. Everyone's fine. Give us a few minutes with them and we'll bring them home." When she hung up, she looked down at my brothers. "What do you want to know about her?"

"This is the Collier family section, so why does it say 'Shay'?" Troy demanded.

Shelby smiled sadly and kneeled down next to them. "Because Annabelle was my daughter," she said.

"And yours?" Will asked me, looking hurt. "How come you never told us? Is that why you left the way you did?"

I started to talk, but Shelby cut me off. "It's not his fault, Will. Until a few days ago he had no idea she even existed, even if only for a short time. And the new carvings were made when I finally told him."

"What happened, Aunt Shelby?" Oscar asked sadly.

"She died in a car accident while I was still pregnant with her. Until this week, no one but Doc ever knew."

The boys all hugged my mate. "I'm sorry you went through that all alone," Troy said.

"You know you're not alone anymore, right?" Will asked. "We're a family now."

"And we would have sealed that officially if you goons hadn't snuck off and scared everyone half to death," I grumbled.

"Oops, sorry," Troy said.

"We'll head back to the house if you want to go home and finish it," Will offered.

Shelby looked up at me and scrunched her nose.

I laughed. "Pretty sure you just put a cold shower stop to that plan, but thanks."

"Come on," Shelby said. "Let's get you three home."

We got the boys into the car and I drove over to the Alpha house. Maddie and Cora were waiting outside for them. With heads hung low, they went to face their punishment.

Liam stepped out to evaluate the scene. "Let me guess, truth or dare?"

Oscar grinned sheepishly up at his father and nodded.

"To the cemetery?" Maddie asked, sounding exasperated. "Really?"

He shrugged. "It sounded good at the time. We weren't planning to spend the night out there. Will got upset, so that's what we ended up doing."

"Will, are you okay?" Cora asked, sounding genuinely concerned. "What happened?"

Shelby shook her head. "Not now, Mom. I'll explain it later. We have it under control."

Maddie stared at her and I watched as something transpired between the sisters.

"You know what? It doesn't matter. You guys are safe and that's all that matters. Come on in and eat breakfast," Maddie finally said.

"Really?" Oscar asked looking from his mother to his father, waiting for one of them to laugh or discipline him or something.

"If that's what your mom said, then go. Don't look a gift horse in the mouth," Liam said.

The boys scurried off into the house while Maddie walked over and hugged Shelby.

"Are you okay?" she asked my mate.

Shelby nodded. "Yeah. We had a talk with them. It's fine."

Cora wiped tears from her cheek. "They found Annabelle's grave, didn't they? I noticed there was a new addition to it made recently."

"I'm not going to apologize for that," I said.

"You knew?" Shelby asked.

Cora started crying and hugged her close. "Of course I knew, but Doc said you were adamant that he tell no one. He had to get permission from your father to bury her in a Collier plot. You seemed to be handling it okay, so I never said anything. We always assumed she was Ben's, but we weren't certain until we saw Shay carved under her name a few days ago. I still visit her often."

"Thank you," Shelby said.

Cora grabbed my arm and pulled me into their hug. "If the two of you can get through something like that, and find your way back to each other, then you can face anything life throws your way. I'm so glad she has you back in her life," she told me.

Later that day the boys had to say goodbye to Oscar as Maddie and Liam headed back to San Marco. I didn't even growl when Walker hugged Shelby goodbye.

When Monday came, Shelby and the twins settled back into their school routine and I was on my own for much of the day. I tried showing up to lunch a few times, but she actually told me I was too much of a distraction.

By Wednesday most of Shelby's things had been moved to the house. She was staying in my room and would be even after I left. My days seemed short and I wasn't ready for Monday to come.

Saturday, I finally got to spend some time alone with Shelby. Cora and Zach had decided to pay a visit to my parents and took Troy and Will with them for the weekend. I wasn't sure how I would ever repay their kindness.

"Alone at last," Shelby said, flopping back onto my couch and reaching for the remote.

I frowned. "I have roughly forty-eight hours left here, and you want to spend it watching television?"

"I was thinking a movie, unless you had something better in mind," she said slyly.

I picked her up as I sat myself down on the couch and lowered her onto my lap. “Actually I do. I thought maybe we could pick up exactly where we were interrupted last weekend.”

I knew she knew what I was asking, and I needed so badly for her to say yes. I couldn’t stand another second without being bonded to her.

She pulled her hair to one side and once again exposed her neck to me. “You mean here?”

I could hear her heartbeat race and knew she was nervous. I hated that she still had hesitations about my intentions being real. I was about to prove to her just how serious I was.

“Exactly,” I said, calling my canines forward. I didn’t even hesitate as I sunk my teeth into her neck. I had already waited far too long.

Shelby moaned and I felt a pinch as she bit into me.

Finally, I thought.

Of course I’d heard about the frenzy that consumes a pair as the bond seals, but I was not at all prepared for the emotional flood it caused, especially with my mate. I felt her warm tears drip onto my shoulder and I knew she was crying. I prayed they were happy tears.

I started to pant and needed her with a desperation I didn’t know possible. I literally ripped the clothes from her body, understanding why bonding and sex tended to go hand in hand. I couldn’t get inside her fast enough.

As she settled down on me, my entire body shuddered with a sense of completeness I had never known. We were one. Neither of us moved as my teeth slowly retracted. I licked the drop of blood on her neck and kissed the mark I’d left with a grin of satisfaction.

She did much the same, and then threw her head back and started to move as if she couldn’t take it one more second. Her eyes locked with mine and never left, until she couldn’t keep them open any longer as she withered in my arms. It felt like a volcano had just erupted inside me as my overheated body released, too.

I laid us down on the couch without a word and tucked her close to my chest.

“Mine,” I said with a newfound fierceness.

“Always,” she replied, kissing my chest where her head lay.

Shelby

Chapter 21

Life felt pretty close to perfect. Ben had finally claimed me and a lot of my fears and concerns about him leaving subsided. Okay, they weren't entirely gone, but dimmed in comparison. He was mine now, always and forever, and officially. I could handle the time apart that we'd be facing, because I knew he couldn't stay away now that we were bonded mates.

That knowledge didn't make his leaving any easier, though. We spent the bulk of the weekend skyping with his family, making love, and finally discussing our future together.

"I'm okay with moving to San Marco," I assured him for the millionth time.

"But I see how much you love teaching here, and I hate that I'm going to take that away from you," Ben said.

"You're not. This is my choice because I have final veto power, remember? Besides, there's children who need good teachers there, too," I told him, recalling a promise he had made to me when he was discussing the job with Patrick.

A part of me was terrified any time he mentioned the job. A sniper? I hated guns and stuff like that, but then I had to force myself to remember that this is what he does. Still, I knew he had been shot at least twice in his nine years of service. That didn't sit well with me, but I would never tell him that.

"Maddie is in Westin, and Lizzy is there half the year. I'll have family around, not to mention friends. We grew up with the Westins, Ben. I'm going to be fine there. Besides, it's only a couple hours flight back home, and I know Thomas will send me the plane anytime I ask."

"I know, I just want you to be certain. No regrets."

"I am certain, and this is only a trial anyway. Maybe it will work out, maybe it won't."

Ben sighed. "There's only so many opportunities for an ex-sniper, Sport. I was lucky to stumble across this one. As much as I hate to admit it, I have Walker to thank for that."

"Admit it, he's growing on you," I teased.

"That little shit really is," he admitted, making us both laugh.

It was Sunday night, or maybe even the wee hours of Monday morning, that we lay in bed talking. Neither of us wanted to close our eyes, knowing the alarm would blast too soon, and Ben would have to leave.

"Are you sure you're okay with the twins?"

"Stop worrying. The boys and I are going to be fine as long as you don't ghost us."

That was still my biggest fear: Ben would leave, and I wouldn't hear from him again for another nine years. I knew in my heart things were different this time and I was just being ridiculous, but that didn't stop the fears and memories from surfacing.

"That's not going to happen. I promise you. We'll video chat every day I'm gone. And it's not like when I left for boot camp and couldn't communicate. I will have my cell phone on me nearly all the time. Chances of me getting called to service will be very slim, and that is the only reason I wouldn't be available."

"Is it going to be hard to walk away?" I asked.

He shrugged. "Maybe a little. I mean, sure, a part of me feels like I'm letting my team down, but they already have me benched indefinitely, so I doubt they'll even be all that surprised. Besides, it will be a lot harder walking away from you tomorrow, than it will be to leave them."

I smiled. "Good answer," I told him.

"When you're with Westin Force will you be gone a lot?" I asked. It was something I'd been wanting to ask for a while but wasn't a hundred percent certain I wanted to know the answer.

"I don't know, Sport, but if it keeps me away from you too much, then we'll reassess. It's only a trial," he reminded me.

I nodded and snuggled closer to him. Looking at the clock on the wall, I knew Thomas would be home with the twins soon. They needed a little time alone with their brother, too.

"When the boys get back, I'm going to go and hang out with Peyton for a few hours and give you some time with them."

"That's not necessary, Shelbs. It's 'us' now, not just 'me'," he said.

"I know that, Ben, but it's not going to be easy on them with you leaving, especially right now, and it will mean everything to them to get a few brotherly hours in before saying goodbye. Trust me on this."

He nodded, but I could tell he didn't like it. I bit back a smile, not wanting him to know how much I liked it that he didn't like it, because that meant he wanted to spend his last moments with me too. We would, but I knew this was too important for his little brothers.

"You could go home and pack the rest of your stuff," he suggested. I knew there wasn't much love there between him and Peyton, but I also wanted to smooth some things over with her. It was really my fault for how much she resented him.

"I would, but Maddie and Liam left yesterday and that means Mom will be in a funk today. I just don't want to deal with it," I confessed.

"Fine," he said. "But can you stay at least until they get back?"

I loved that he didn't want me to leave and I readily agreed. We made slow, lazy love one last time, taking our time, knowing it may be our last opportunity to be alone together for a while.

Thomas called when the plane's wheels touched down and I reluctantly got dressed while Ben jumped in the shower. I considered joining him, but that had the potential to lead to a very awkward start for me and the twins.

I did poke my head in long enough to give him a quick kiss before heading out.

When I got to Peyton's, I let myself in without even knocking.

"Hey, Shelby," Kenneth said. "Peyton's putting Eve down for her nap right now. She'll be down in a few minutes. I'm heading out to work on the greenhouse over at the diner."

"Thanks, Kenneth. See you later," I said.

I waited around downstairs for about fifteen minutes with no sign of Peyton. I climbed the stairs quietly, wondering if it really took that long to put the baby down. The nursery door was closed, but I knew there was a second entrance through the back of the closet in my sister's room, so I tried there next. Instead, I found Peyton passed out and snoring in her bed.

With a frown, I climbed in beside her and lay down next to her. I had been doing that since we were children, so I really didn't think anything of it.

The snoring stopped and she smiled before opening her eyes.

"Are you still mad at me?" she asked.

"What? Why would I be mad at you?"

"Because I've been a bitch to your mate, and I blabbed your secrets, making me the world's worst sister ever."

She rolled to her side to look at me.

"I'm not mad. I needed to talk about those things. You just gave me the uncomfortable push to do it."

"I didn't know about Annabelle. I'm so sorry, Shelbs."

I smiled sadly. "It was something I've been carrying alone for so long, Pey. I don't know, opening up and sharing her with Ben sort of freed me from that burden and I wanted to share her with all of you."

"But I feel horrible," she said.

"What?"

"Because all Lily and I go on about is wanting to be pregnant, and here you can't get pregnant and it's just so unfair."

"It doesn't bother me, you know. I mean, hearing you guys talk and playing with the babies. I love my nieces," I told her. "I think not being able to have kids of my own makes me love them even more."

"There are other ways to grow a family, you know," she said. "I mean, I didn't actually give birth to my daughter, but I'd rip out anyone's throat who tried to argue that she isn't mine."

"I know. Ben mentioned that too, but let's be honest, how many little shifter babies are just lying around awaiting adoption? It wouldn't be fair to bring a human child into our life, so that's a pretty big long shot that I'm not willing to get my hopes up on."

Peyton sighed. "I know. Want me to be a surrogate for you guys? I mean, that could be doable."

I laughed. "Thanks, I'll keep that in mind, but honestly I've come to terms with the fact that I'll never be a mom. As long as Ben can live with that, we'll be fine. Plus I get to spoil my nieces and nephews all that much more."

We lay there and talked for a few hours until my phone started buzzing impatiently. I picked up and looked at the screen, not at all surprised to see multiple text messages all saying the same thing: Come home!

"Looks like Ben and the boys have had enough brotherly bonding and are ready for me to come home," I laughed.

When I moved to sit up, Peyton noticed my new bond mark and grinned. "He finally claimed you!"

My hand flew to my neck and I nodded. "He said he was going to before he left. Cut that one a little close, but honestly since Mom and Dad took the boys for the weekend, it was our first truly alone time in the last two weeks. We've had moments here and there, but always with the possibility of interruptions. According to Ben, that was the only reason he had waited."

"Well, I'm glad it's done, and he's already returning to my good graces for it."

I laughed. "I'm sure he'll be relieved to hear it."

"I have an extra casserole in the fridge, why don't you take it home for the boys?" she offered.

"Sure, that would be great."

I followed Peyton downstairs to the kitchen and graciously accepted her offer. Just as I was leaving, Eve started crying.

I smiled. "Yup, I'm okay with being able to walk away from that."

Peyton groaned as I left and drove back to the Shays' house.

"I come bearing food," I said as I walked in without knocking. It felt a little bit weird, but I figured I might as well get used to it, since that would be home for the unforeseeable future.

Will ran over and sniffed the casserole as he took it. "What is it?"

"I don't know. Didn't ask. Something Peyton gave me."

"Peyton made it?" Troy asked.

"Yes," I confirmed.

The boys high fived each other.

"Woohoo, we know it's going to be good then," Will said.

We had a nice, lighthearted meal, just the four of us, before they got ready for bed and told Ben goodbye.

"Are you sure you want to go to school and not to the airport tomorrow?" I asked them for the hundredth time.

"Yeah, we think it's best. You gave us time with him tonight and we really appreciate it. We'd rather just say goodbye and have a normal day," Troy said.

"Yup, you two can have the sloppy, tearful goodbye all by yourselves," Will said, rolling his eyes.

"If you change your mind. . ."

"We know, Shelby. We know," Will said.

The boy hugged Ben again. "We'll say goodbye before we leave for school."

"I've got a substitute lined up for the day. Go easy on her, please, and don't forget you're riding the bus home tomorrow," I reminded them.

"We'll be fine, Shelby," Troy said. "Goodnight."

Ben and I spent our final night together up late, talking and just holding each other close. I was determined to be strong for him and not let my fears dampen our last moments together.

I woke up exhausted the next morning to make sure the boys ate breakfast and got off to school okay. Ben strolled out at the last minute to say his final goodbyes. Troy had tears in his eyes when he left, but I knew they were going to be okay.

"What time is your flight?" I asked.

"Eleven, so I don't have much time this morning. I feel like I should stop by the Alpha house and tell Thomas and your parents goodbye."

I nodded, selfishly wanting to keep him all to myself, but I knew we had other responsibilities, too.

He showered and dressed as I fought the desire to join him. When he stepped out dressed in uniform and carrying his duffle bag, my breath hitched. He looked so sexy in uniform that I was struggling not to rip it off him.

I licked my lips and groaned, making him beam with pride.

He ushered me out quickly, knowing he would miss his flight if I had my way.

When we got to the Alpha house, Mom hugged him close and cried as she said goodbye. We made our rounds through the house, ending with Thomas.

"Thank you for all you've done for me and my family," Ben told Thomas.

My brother hugged him. "Dude, we're pack, but we're family, too. There's nothing within my power I wouldn't do for you."

"One favor?" Ben asked.

"Of course, anything."

He looked down at me. "Check on Shelby and make sure she actually laughs while I'm gone."

Thomas nodded, and shook Ben's hand. "I'll make it my personal mission," Thomas said evilly.

I groaned and rolled my eyes.

Ben was quiet as I drove him over to the airstrip. We arrived a few minutes before eleven and the plane was ready and waiting.

I blew out a long breath. "Guess it's time," I said.

"It's going to be different this time, Sport. I promise you," he said.

"I know," I told him honestly. I had no doubt this time would be different. "The boys and I are going to be fine. I don't want you worrying about us."

"I'm always going to worry about you. Do me a favor?"

"Anything," I promised.

"Write me every day," he surprised me by saying.

"You want me to mail them or save them for when you return?"

He laughed. "Mail them, woman."

"We do have email and texts now," I reminded him.

He shook his head. "Not the same."

"I promise to write and actually send them in the mail," I said. It made me ridiculously happy that the letters I'd written all those years truly meant that much to him. "We'll video chat, too, though, right?"

"As often as possible."

We hesitantly got out of the car and walked to the plane. The pilot met us at the bottom.

"The chair is already secured. I'll take your bag, sir," he said. "Shelby, will you be joining us today?"

"No, I'm afraid not. We'll say goodbye here," I informed him.

"Take your time. We'll leave when you're ready," the pilot told Ben before heading into the plane to give us some privacy.

"I guess this is it," I said, nervously rocking back and forth on my heels.

Ben raised his hand and gently rubbed my cheek, holding me like I was the most precious thing in his world. He slowly lowered his head to kiss me, taking my breath away. I was so determined not to cry. I wanted to be strong with him, but he was breaking down my resolve with his sweet kisses.

I hugged him so tightly and wasn't certain I could pry myself away from him.

"I love you," I told him.

"I love you," he told me.

He looked up towards the plane and I knew the moment I'd dreaded since the moment I laid eyes on him had finally come.

"It's going to be different this time, Sport. You'll see," he assured me.

With one last kiss, he broke away and forced himself to walk up the stairs.

I stood there waving until the plane was in the air, then I drove back to his house, curled up in a ball, and cried myself to sleep.

When I woke up, I showered and changed, then I made two peanut butter and jelly sandwiches and waited with a smile for the boys to come home. I was determined to not be sad and add additional stress to the twins, who were dealing with enough already.

Just before the bus pulled up, my phone rang with an incoming video chat.

I smiled and swiped my phone to accept.

"Miss me already?" I asked Ben.

"Just landed in Casper and waiting for the next leg of my trip. It'll take a few flights, maybe even a few days before I get back to base, but I'll keep you updated, because I'm going to prove to you that I mean it whenever I say that this time will be different."

When the boys came in, I had just hung up from talking with Ben and was deliriously happy. I no longer had doubts, and sensed that everything was very much different this time.

Ben

Chapter 22

"Welcome home, you bastard!" Bulldog greeted me as I rolled my chair into the bunker.

"Missed me, did ya?" I countered.

"I sure as hell did. I can't believe you just dropped me off and then left me with these monsters," Jake whined.

"Heard you were fitting in just fine around here," I told him.

"Damn straight I am!"

"What the hell is this I'm hearing about you leaving?" Crawley asked. I knew he wouldn't be happy about it.

"You heard right, I'm afraid. Talked to Collins, and he's getting me a full medical discharge. Writing up the paperwork as we speak, though I insisted on coming back to at least say goodbye to you assholes," I told him honestly. It had taken another two weeks to get things sorted and back to my unit, but I was here and that was all that mattered for the moment.

"You're really leaving the army?" Bulldog asked.

"Yeah, I really am. I think Collins is a bit relieved. It's a lot easier to pull the medical discharge card than to sell a miraculous recovery and fit for duty."

"What are you going to do?" Mike asked.

"Not certain yet. There's a group of paramilitary shifters that approached me for an interview. I think I'm going to check them out."

"Westin Force is recruiting you?" Crawley asked.

I nodded, not all that surprised that he was familiar with them.

"I've served a few joint missions with Silas Granger in the past. I hear he's over there now. He's a good man. A hard-ass, and a damn veggie-eating gorilla, but I think you'll like working with him. He ain't as pretty to look at as me, of course," Crawley said.

Everyone hooted with laughter.

"You guys ever consider leaving here, look me up and I'll be happy to hook you up with them," I said.

"We're going to hold you to that," Bulldog said as he grabbed me by the neck and gave me a noogie.

"Yeah, yeah, yeah, I'm going to miss you guys, too."

My phone rang and I smiled as I looked down.

"Bloody hell. I know that look. You've been taken by a dame. That's the real reason you're leaving us," Crawley challenged.

I shrugged, not denying it, and swiped to answer the video call. My heart swelled with joy at the sight of my beautiful mate.

"Hey babe," I said.

"Just wanted to make sure you arrived safe and sound," she said.

"Shit! It really is all because of a woman," Crawley said.

I laughed. "Guys, meet Shelby. Shelby, this Crawley, Mike, Bulldog, and Jake. The others are out at the moment, so I 'll have to show you off to them later," I said as I passed the phone around for each of the guys to say hi to her.

"Wait, Shelby? The dead girl?" Bulldog asked, and Crawley smacked him upside the head.

"I told ya she ain't dead. No man is going to pine after a dead woman for as long as he has her," Crawley said.

Shelby laughed, completely unaffected. "Definitely not dead."

"So what? You went home and reconnected with your old sweetheart?" Mike asked.

I pulled the collar of my uniform down and showed them my mark. "Reconnected with my true mate, who also happens to be my old sweetheart," I said proudly.

"Westin Force won't take ya with a mate, I'm afraid," Crawley said

"They made an exception on a trial basis," I said. I wasn't about to tell them that I had negotiated some fifty vials of memory serum off the major in exchange for that exception.

"Nope, not buying it. Why would they?" Mike asked.

I grinned. "Shelby's a Collier. She has some pretty tight connections with Westin Pack. It pays to be a wolf with a sexy mate, what can I say?" I joked.

Shelby laughed. "I'm pretty sure I did not have anything to do with this."

"No, that makes sense, actually," Mike agreed.

I shrugged. "I'll take it, whatever their reasons."

"Hey, the boys want to say a quick hi, then we have to go. They just got out of basketball practice and we're heading over to have dinner with my parents," Shelby said before Troy took the phone from her.

Some of the guys looked over my shoulder.

"Damn, he looks just like a little miniature version of you," Jake noted.

I smiled. "Yeah, he does. This is Troy. Say hi to the guys, Troy."

"Hey," he said.

"Everything's still okay?" I asked.

"We're fine. Mom and Dad said they should be out in time for Christmas. We're hoping you'll be home this year for it, too."

I hated to disappoint them. "It's not looking very promising, but I'll try," I told him.

Will grabbed the phone from him, and as I listened to them argue about it, made me long to be home. Shelby scolded them both for wasting my time.

"Guys, this is my other brother, Will," I said, wondering why this was the first time I'd ever thought to introduce them. It's not like I hadn't been in contact with my family all these years, even if I was avoiding Shelby.

"Wassup?" Will said. "Do me a favor and don't get him killed before we get him back."

Mike laughed. "And that one sounds just like you."

I laughed too. "Twins: one inherited my good looks, the other my charismatic personality."

"So basically he just said, your twin is ugly, and you're an asshole," Crawley told Will.

"Dude, he's twelve," I told Crawley, though I shouldn't be surprised. We had once rescued a school of young girls and he'd offered a group of them cigarettes to shut them up. It was clearly obvious he had no business ever being around kids.

"Ben, Shelby's telling me to wrap this up, so I just need you to know what you've gotten yourself into," he said seriously. "Shelby can't cook. I mean like at all! You'd think having the same genes as Peyton we'd be eating well, but if it wasn't for her mom and takeout, she'd literally starve us to death."

"Give me that," Shelby said, taking the phone back from him. "Don't listen to them. I can cook just fine," she insisted.

"She burnt the spaghetti last night," Will yelled in the background and I knew it was true because Shelby's cheeks flushed red.

"Don't worry, Shelby," Mike said over my shoulder. "Shay's actually pretty decent in the kitchen. He won't let you starve."

Shelby covered her face with one hand in embarrassment. "I'm not that bad," she insisted.

I laughed. "Doesn't matter to me," I assured her.

"We have to get going," she said reluctantly. "Can I call tomorrow?"

"Call anytime. If he doesn't answer it's because I took his phone. He's still on my watch until those papers clear," Crawley said. "But you seem sweet, so I'll try to go easy on him."

"Uh, thanks, Crawley. I think," she said.

"Talk to you tomorrow," I told her. "Love you."

The boys obnoxiously started hooting and hollering and making kissy noises in the background as I shoved the closest one away and shook my head as she waved bye and disconnected.

"So what's a mate? And what's the mark on your neck you showed off before she called?" Jake asked.

The others groaned.

"You explain it, Shay, since you're the pansy who got yourself into that mess," Crawley said as the others dispersed quickly.

I sighed when Jake sat down next to me, genuinely curious.

"Fine. It's a shifter thing, kind of like a marriage, only much more permanent."

"How so?" he asked.

"Well, legend goes that God gave each shifter one true mate. We can have lots of compatible mates, but only ever one true mate. There are signs that help direct you toward her, and once you get together, a bond is formed. They say you can walk away from a true mate, but I honestly have never met anyone who successfully did."

"So you basically have no say in the matter?"

"Sort of, but imagine one person created specifically for you, absolute perfection. Why wouldn't you want that?"

"Fair enough, but say you didn't," he challenged.

"Well, like I said, there are supposedly ways to break the bond, but I don't know about all that, because nothing made me happier to find out Shelby was mine."

"You really love her," Jake noted.

"I've loved that girl my entire life. Only reason I ever joined the army is because I didn't think she was mine. If I had known she was my one true mate, I'd never have been able to walk away from her."

He nodded. "I can appreciate that. I joined right after my girlfriend and I broke up. Needed to get as far away from her as possible," he admitted.

"It was something like that," I said, still hating that I'd lost nine years together with her over a stupid lie.

"So what's the mark part?"

"It's a shifter thing," I said. "It seals the bond between us, marks her as mine, and this is where she marked me as hers. Our bond will only continue to grow, and it gives us certain powers as it strengthens. For example, you know I went home because my dad shattered his leg. Well, he and my mom are fully bonded mates. She feels everything he feels, and if he had died, so would she. They can also speak to each other telepathically. It'll still be years before Shelby and I reach that stage."

Jake looked horrified. "That's a good thing?"

"Yeah. Why would I ever want to live without her? A full bond ensures I'll never have to. If she dies, I'll peacefully follow her to the afterlife."

"That is some messed up shit," he said.

I laughed and shrugged. "Like I said, it's a shifter thing."

"Morbid curiosity has me asking just how you mark each other," he said, sounding uncertain about really wanting the answer.

I called my canines forward and grinned at him then snapped my teeth together. Jake nearly jumped off the bed as I laughed.

"She bit you? You bit her?" he asked, disgusted.

I grinned, retracting my teeth. "The bond requires a blood exchange," I confessed.

"I think I'm going to be sick," he said, making gagging noises.

"It's really not as bad as you're thinking."

"All caught up on the birds and the bees there, sweet cheeks? Because we have work to do," Crawley walked over to say.

"What's the mission?" I asked.

"Sorry, old friend, but I have specific orders to keep your ass benched. No action for you until you get home safe and sound to that pretty little mate of yours."

"Crawley, don't do this. I'm here. I can help."

"Wish I could, Ben. There's no one I trust to have my back more, but I'm afraid they've pulled rank on me and unlike you, I still plan to stick around here for a few more decades."

I nodded. "Yes, sir. I understand. I don't like it, but I do get it. Stay safe. I'll behave."

"Wow. You must really be in love, because honestly I thought we were going to have to knock you out and tie you up to keep you here," Crawley laughed.

"I do, and that's not necessary. I'm out," I said. There was only a mild sting of guilt as I said it. I knew it was time for me to move on.

Much to my surprise, a few hours after they left, Major Collins showed up personally. My papers were in order and I was officially being discharged of service. It was all happening so fast, it was making my head spin.

"Why the hell did you send me back here if it was coming up this fast?" I asked.

Jeff shrugged. "Just thought you needed to tell them in person and say goodbye."

I nodded. "Only half the team was here though."

"I'm sorry about that, but you are officially no longer my problem," he said, handing me my final orders and escorting me to the plane waiting to take us home. "Wait, where's your chair?"

I laughed, and then groaned. "You're serious?"

"I just got you one hundred percent medical disability. Hell yes, you're going to ride out in that chair. Don't blow it now," he warned.

"Yes, sir," I said, taking a seat and driving my electric chair out. The men awaiting us struggled to get me and the chair up the ramp, and I just sat there and let them while trying not to laugh. If only they knew.

We were in the air for about two hours when the call came through. It was a call that would haunt me for the rest of my life. I didn't know what was being said, but I knew from the look on Collins' face that it was bad.

He hung up and looked over at me.

"What?" I demanded.

"Your unit. They didn't stand a chance. It was a setup. I'm so sorry," he said.

My heart fell. "How bad?"

"I don't know."

"How bad, Collins?" I yelled.

"Early reports look like three survivors."

"Three? What the hell happened?"

"I don't know. I don't know," he said, and I could tell he was clearly just as upset.

"Who made it?" I asked. I had to know.

"Crawley, Jake, and Bulldog were medevacked out, but early reports say they're stable."

"That's it?" I asked, feeling the bile rise in my chest.

"I'm afraid so, son."

I leaned over the side of my chair and vomited. They were all gone? It was too much to comprehend. I had just seen Mike a few hours ago. He was fine. He had to be fine.

"I'm so sorry," Major Collins said.

Shelby

Chapter 23

It had been four days since I last heard from Ben. He looked happy and promised we'd talk the next day. I couldn't help the panic that set in, worried he was ghosting me once again. The boys asked about him every day and I lied and told them he was just busy wrapping things up and he'd be home as soon as he could, but I didn't know if that was true or not.

I wanted to trust him. I wanted to believe that true love could conquer all, and I had no doubts that Ben loved me. But I literally felt despair through our bond, and it scared me. I couldn't help but fear the worst. Either he had changed his mind and wasn't coming home, or something bad had happened.

I tried to distract us all by taking the boys out to find and cut down the perfect Christmas tree. We decorated the entire house. We burnt cookies on our first attempt and called Peyton over to assist with the second.

By the time we finally got good news that Marnie and Don were heading home, it looked like Christmas had puked on the Shay house.

"Shelby, it's beautiful," Marnie said, hugging me happily.

"We've got a lot to celebrate this year. It's going to be the best Christmas ever," Don said, putting a smile on for the boys' sakes.

I knew from Thomas's updates that Don was suffering from severe depression. Seeing him for myself, even while he tried to fake otherwise, reminded me of how Ben seemed to be feeling and I suddenly knew, something was very wrong.

After packing my bags and hugging everyone goodbye, I left for them to spend time together healing as a family.

I drove home but stopped by a favorite overlook at the river and sat in the car and cried. I pulled out my phone to call Ben. Instead, I sent him a text, afraid he still wouldn't answer once again.

ME: I know something's wrong. I can feel it. Please just talk to me.

I had only been texting him happy stories about the boys and pictures of our Christmas decorating adventures, trying not to let him know I was freaking out, but that was exactly what was happening. As I sat there letting my fears and worries sink in, my heart started racing and I struggled to breathe.

I was heading towards a full-blown panic attack when the phone rang.

Tears sprang to my eyes as I looked down and saw Ben's picture requesting a video chat. With a shaky hand, I slid to accept.

He looked rougher than the last time I saw him. He was sporting a days-old beard, his hair was unkempt, and there were dark circles under his eyes.

"Sport, what's wrong?" he asked.

"Ben?" I asked, fearing I was hallucinating during my panic attack.

"I need you to breathe, babe. In and out. You have to calm down and tell me what happened," he said a little too calmly.

Anger replaced my panic. "I don't hear from you for nearly a week and you're asking me what's wrong? How the hell am I supposed to know? I can feel you, Ben. I know something is wrong, but you won't talk to me. So don't sit there and calmly ask me what's happening, 'cause I don't have a clue. It sure feels a hell of a lot like boot camp all over again," I said, feeling equally better and guiltier over getting that off my chest.

He sighed and looked so defeated. "I'm sorry. I've been so busy just trying to survive this week, I didn't even think of how it would affect you. Shit," he said, running a hand through his slightly shaggy hair. "You kept sending pics of you and the boys and you looked so happy that I didn't want to drag you down over the holidays."

"What the hell is that supposed to mean?"

"The last time we video chatted, well, Major Collins showed up shortly after to give me my release papers."

"Wait, you've been out for a week? And you what, decided you're just not coming back?" I asked, trying not to work myself up to hyperventilating. I wasn't going to give him the satisfaction.

"It's not like that. Would you just let me finish? Yes, I've officially been out for the last week, but that same night my team got called up. I wasn't allowed to join them, but there was a . . . it was really bad, Shelby," he said, and I suddenly noticed the red rim around his eyes. Had he been crying? Ben took a deep breath and continued. "Only three survived, two of them are still fighting for their lives. I've been at the hospital just waiting and praying for days. To be honest, I don't even have a clue what today it is. Jake's here, too. We're both a mess as we await word. They took Crawley back for a third surgery today. Even his, um, gifts, aren't helping him heal, Shelbs. And Bulldog just got stabilized yesterday."

"Why didn't you just tell me, Ben? We're supposed to be there for each other through the good and the bad."

"I know. I just didn't want to burden you with all this around the holidays. I know you're trying to wrap up school and I couldn't add more stress on you for that. Plus, you've already got so much on your plate stepping up to take care of my brothers. I know I'm shit for not running home to help. I just, I just really need to be here right now," he said.

"Of course you do," I told him. "They're your brothers, too. And Troy and Will and I have done just fine. Your parents came home today, so I'm giving them some space and time alone."

"Is that why you were so upset and going into a panic attack? It was so weird, like I could feel you before your text came through, and I knew I had to call you," he admitted.

"That's called the bond, Ben, and you're a giant idiot! I've been feeling your turmoil of emotions for the last week as clear as if they were my own. I've tried to reach out, but you continue to ignore me, so I'm left here to think the absolute worse, and while your friends dying is absolutely horrible, it's nowhere near the worst-case scenario my imagination can come up with. I just needed to know you were okay and not lying in a ditch dying alone somewhere."

I hated the additional pain I was causing him. I could see it on his face and feel it through the bond.

"I'm so sorry, Shelby. I had no idea you could feel all that. I just didn't want to burden you with all this, too," he said, and I knew he genuinely meant it. In some warped way he was just trying to protect me.

"I get that, Ben, but things are different now. You can't just hide something like that or ghost me and think everything's going to be okay."

"I know. I'm actually stateside, but I just can't leave until I know Crawley's going to be okay."

"Is it safe there? We could try to get him transferred over to where your parents are," I said.

"Um, that's where he is already," Ben confessed.

"Oh," I said, not knowing how to handle that. "Your parents didn't mention that."

"That's because I didn't visit them," he said softly. "I just couldn't, Shelbs. They have enough on their plates without worrying about me, too."

I didn't even know what to say to that. He was only a short flight away and hadn't said anything to me, but to be in the same building as his parents and not even check in on them was something I just could not fathom.

"I know in a way I've been selfish, but honestly, I'm just trying to get through this. It's hard," he said, and the turmoil in his voice nearly broke my heart.

"I have two days left of school before break. Do you want me to come?"

"You'd do that?" he asked.

"Yes, you idiot," I said. I felt relief and happiness expand through our bond. "Did you really think I wouldn't want to be there with you?" I asked before I could stop myself.

"I don't know," he said honestly. "I knew I couldn't handle you saying no if I asked you to, and I knew you were already tied up with my brothers and school and everything. I couldn't bring myself to ask."

I was so frustrated with him, but I knew he was hurting and needed me.

We hung up and he promised to call and check in every day, no matter what.

The next morning I arrived to work early and headed straight to the main office. I didn't waste any time giving my final notice. I didn't explain much, just told them that I wouldn't be staying in Collier much longer. I knew they would find a good replacement or realign the classes to cover mine with no issues. I'm sure it wasn't the top thing on anyone's holiday list, but I had to move on.

"You're certain about this?" my boss asked.

I nodded. "Yes, and I'm so sorry. Different circumstances and I'd have probably stayed here teaching forever. I love it, but I love my mate more and our life together is leading away from Collier."

With no more ties to cut, I had a few phone calls to make, and then my parents and sisters to face. I asked them all to come to dinner the next night. When Peyton learned I was planning on cooking, she begged me to spare everyone's stomachs and let her do it. Of course, I'd been counting on that already and readily agreed.

I made certain the dampener was on in my bedroom as I called Maddie.

"Hey Shelbs, give me two minutes," she whispered. I could tell she laid the phone down and could hear rustling on the other end before she returned. "Sorry about that. I was just putting Sara down when you called. What's up?"

"You know about the offer Patrick made to Ben, right?"

"Yeah, he's due to report next week actually. Did you decide to come with him? We weren't sure since Ben insisted on a trial period."

"I'm coming, but I need to make arrangements for a place to live during this trial.

"Done, with options," Maddie said. "Liam and I have already been discussing this. You're welcome to stay at the lodge, but there's also a small vacant house just down the road from us. We'd be neighbors!" she exclaimed. "Not that I'm pressuring your decision in any way. It's a three-bedroom rancher, nothing fancy, but if you like the location and decide to stay long term, you could always rebuild on that site."

"That sounds perfect, actually," I said, thinking of the benefits of living next door to my sister and getting to watch my niece and nephew grow up. "I love that idea. Thanks! I'll reach out to Kyle to get approval."

"Do that, but it's already been sorted. He knows Ben's coming and already gave permission should you come with him."

"Your doing?"

"Maybe," she said. "I'm trying not to get too excited, but I love the idea of you being here. Having Lizzy half the year is great, but she's always so busy and so caught up in Cole that I barely see her when she's here."

"I've struggled a little with the thought of leaving Collier, but having you there definitely helps soften the blow."

"When are you coming?"

"I don't know. I'll see Ben tomorrow and we'll discuss it. He's going through some shit right now and trying to handle everything on his own. I just want to show him he doesn't have to anymore."

"So you're lining up the move, and then telling him about it?"

"Basically," I confessed.

She laughed. "You're crazy, and I love you. Can't wait to see you soon. I know it's all going to work out no matter what he's going through right now, because you guys aren't just mates but best friends. Remember that and you'll be just fine."

We hung up and I quickly called Kyle. Being so late, I chanced calling him at home.

"Hello?" a female voice answered.

"Kelsey?" I asked

"Yes, who's this?"

"It's Shelby Collier," I said.

"Shelby! I was wondering when we were going to hear from you. Maddie's been busy lining up housing and relocation plans for you and your new mate. It's all she talks about right now. She is so excited to have you here."

"She's the best," I admitted. "That's actually why I'm calling. Ben's been a bit tied up dealing with a tragic accident from his old unit, and I don't know how much of all of this he's had time to deal with. Maddie says there's a house next door to her available, but that's most definitely in Westin territory."

"Kyle's already approved it, but I know you'll feel better hearing it from him. Hold on," she said.

"Shelby?" Kyle asked as he took the phone.

"Hey, Kyle."

"Everything's good. You and Ben are welcome in Westin territory anytime and I have no problems with you taking over the vacancy. I hate having a good house just sit there."

"Thank you so much, Kyle."

"Do you have a move-in date yet?"

"No, but I'm meeting up with Ben tomorrow and will figure that out. I just wanted to get everything in order first. He's been dealing with a lot and I'm not sure how much he's managed to line up."

"Yeah, he's been minimally in touch with Patrick, enough that we're aware of the situation and send our condolences. I pray his friends pull through. I won't lie, we're a little concerned with his mental capacity to take on a new unit right now. Maybe he needs a little downtime first."

"I'll talk to him and let you know for sure, but I think moving on right now would do him some good. A new focus will help him push through his funk."

"I can certainly appreciate that, too. Keep in touch and let us know what you decide."

"Thanks, Kyle. Talk to you soon," I said, hanging up the phone.

I took a quick shower and my phone was ringing when I got out. I smiled when I saw it was Ben. We talked for about an hour. His friend Bulldog was doing much better and Crawley was finally stabilized. I could see his relief and feel the stress melt from him. I didn't tell him about my talks with Kyle and Maddie though, or that I had quit my job. There would be time for that when I saw him in person.

I went to bed feeling better than I had in a week.

My final day of classes was harder than I thought. I made it a fun day with a holiday party for each class followed by a tearful goodbye. I had worked hard to wrap up all outstanding grades and surprised them with no assignments over the holiday break. I didn't feel it was fair to have stuff hanging out there for the new replacement to clean up.

When my final class walked in, it was with long, gloomy faces.

"Word already spread, huh?" I asked them.

"You're really quitting?" Caroline asked.

"I'm afraid I am," I admitted.

"But you're like the greatest teacher we've ever had," John complained.

"Thank you, but as you grow up, you'll realize that sometimes these decisions are out of your control," I said.

"But it is your decision. Ben would be okay with you staying here," Troy insisted.

"It's only a trial job, right?" Will asked.

I sighed. "It's a trial that we hope works out for good."

Troy looked devastated. "But that means my brother's never coming back to live in Collier?"

I walked over and hugged him. "Troy, Ben hasn't been here for a long time. This isn't his home anymore. He has to go where he's needed, and this job is a really important one. Besides, it's only in Westin Pack."

"That's half a country away," Will pointed out.

"That's a couple hours flight away. No way are we just disappearing from your lives," I insisted.

"Just ours," John said.

"It's not like that, John. I will always be a Collier first and foremost and I'll be home to visit pretty regularly. And that means checking in on you to make sure you aren't giving your next teacher too hard a time."

The class laughed.

"This is a really good thing, you guys. And it's the last day of school before Christmas break, so let's stop moping and celebrate!"

Even Will and Troy perked up a little by the end of the day. I drove them home, got out the big box of presents from the trunk of my car, and walked in with them.

"What's all this?" Marnie asked.

"An early Christmas treat," I said with a big a smile.

"You sorted things out with Ben, I take it."

"Maybe. I'm flying out to meet up with him tomorrow. We haven't set an official move date yet, but they are anxious to get him started on his trial period over at Westin Force. I have everything else lined up for the move and am feeling better about it," I admitted.

"Today was her last day of school. She quit," Troy pouted.

I reached over and hugged him. Something I had wanted to do in class but hadn't dared.

"I keep telling you, you aren't getting rid of me that easily."

Will helped me carry the packages into the living room.

"Hi Don, how are you feeling?"

"Good," he said. "It's a real good day. I'm happy to be home."

I still worried about him, but he was strong, and I had to have faith that he'd get through this.

I sat down on the floor and passed out gifts.

"Shelby, shouldn't we wait until Christmas? I haven't even had time to shop yet," Marnie confessed.

I smiled. "That's up to you guys. I'm fine either way. Since I don't know where I'll be for Christmas, I just wanted to make sure I delivered these."

"Let's put them under the tree," Will said.

"Yeah, no matter what's happening, Ben's never missed a Christmas," Troy said.

I was surprised to hear that. To the best of my knowledge he'd not been back home before his return the week of Thanksgiving.

"He always video calls in for Christmas morning," Don said.

"Oh, I didn't know that."

"It's tradition, so no matter where life takes the two of you, we will always celebrate the holiday together," he said.

I smiled. "I like that." I turned to Will and Troy. "So, no shaking the presents."

They both grinned. "Yeah, sure," they said together.

I apologized for having to cut the visit short with the Shays, but I also had a family dinner to attend.

Everyone was already there when I arrived, and the house smelled wonderfully of Peyton's cooking. I walked in and smiled. My mother had tears in her eyes, and I realized they already knew.

Ben

Chapter 24

I woke up early, truly excited for the day. I had tried to take on the world alone and shelter Shelby from my pain, but as she came in like a tornado just a few days ago and tore down all the barriers I'd put up between work and my personal life, I quickly realized that she would always take away that darkness I was facing if I just let her in.

Once Crawley was finally stable, his recovery came quickly. Bulldog too, who admitted to complaining just enough to keep him there until he knew Crawley was okay. I wasn't at all surprised about it. Jake had stayed by my side through it all. I had to admit, the kid had definitely grown on me.

They were all home for the holidays now on personal leave, but I knew that with the new year would come a new team, stronger and better than the last, because at the end of the day, no matter what, the Ghosts would live on, even without me.

I knew Shelby was showing up at the hospital, but I hadn't expected her to come having already walked away from her home. She had made all the arrangements, cleared our passage into Westin, and even had a house lined up for us.

When I had asked her if she was certain about leaving her home she'd laughed in my face.

"I'm not leaving my home, Ben. I'm finally coming home, because where you are, that's home to me," she had said.

I smiled at the memory and rolled over to try to get out of bed, which caused a wave that instantly woke Shelby up laughing.

"Maybe an air mattress wasn't my most brilliant idea," she admitted in a deep, husky morning voice that I loved.

We had spent Christmas Eve day traveling to our next adventure in life and settling into a small house in San Marco. It felt a little strange to be in Westin territory, but not as bad as I had predicted, at least not yet.

Shelby had made me stop by a store at the final city before making our way up the mountain to our new home. She had purchased only a handful of things: an air mattress to sleep on; a coffee pot and coffee fixings; two mugs; a cookie sheet; a pack of cinnamon rolls; and, a small Christmas tree that came with decorations.

Aside from our suitcases, they were our only possessions. The house felt huge, though I was confident my mate would soon fill each room to perfection. I liked that it gave her something to do in the days ahead because my first assignment with Bravo company of Westin Force was coming up fast. I was scheduled to meet the team officially on New Year's Eve.

I managed to get up and headed for the bathroom. After doing my business and cleaning up a little, I walked out to the smell of freshly brewing coffee and found Shelby in the kitchen humming Christmas carols as she worked on laying out the cinnamon rolls.

I wrapped my arms around her waist and kissed the mark on her neck. She sighed.

"I'm just about done here, but it's probably too early to video message the boys. So what do you want to do in the meantime?" she asked as she wiggled her sexy behind against me.

I could think of a million ways we still needed to christen every room in the house, but there would be plenty of time for that. Looking at the time, I knew without a doubt she was wrong. I was surprised the boys hadn't already called us.

"You're a tease, and I promise you they are up and waiting for us."

"You think?"

"I know. The sun's up, so they've been up for a while already," I said with a chuckle.

Shelby scrunched up her nose and turned in my arms to face me. "I've spent two weeks with them, and they never wake up before the sun," she insisted.

"For school. This is different, it's Christmas." I leaned down and kissed her, holding her tightly to me. "Merry Christmas, Shelby."

She grinned up at me. "Merry Christmas, Ben."

Right on cue, my phone rang.

I groaned. "Told ya."

Shelby grabbed it from me and swiped to answer. "Merry Christmas!"

"Merry Christmas, Shelby," the twins said in unison.

"Is Ben there too?" Troy asked.

"I'm here, buddy," I said.

Shelby headed into our new living room to sit on the floor in front of the pathetic Charlie Brown-esque Christmas tree we'd thrown together before bed.

I made a mental note to at least borrow a few camp chairs or something to sit on until we had time to buy some furniture. For now, I joined my mate on the floor and leaned close to watch the festivities back home on the small screen of my phone.

One by one, they opened presents I had left.

"Shelby, can I open this one from you and Ben next?" Will asked.

"That one is for the both of you. Open it with Troy," she instructed.

I didn't even know Shelby had gotten them gifts, let alone marked them from both of us. I kissed her temple, feeling overwhelmingly grateful to have her back in my life.

I watched the boys open the gift and freak out in excitement. I couldn't even tell what it was.

"What is it?"

"It's a drone!" they screamed together.

"You have to share it though. No fighting," Shelby added.

"You bought them a drone?"

She shrugged. "I wanted something they could do together."

"You're amazing," I told her.

She looked up and smiled as I closed the gap and kissed her. The boys were too absorbed with their new toy to even notice.

We hung out on the phone a few more minutes as the last of the presents were opened before saying goodbye to the boys and my parents.

"Is that how Christmas always is for you?" she asked.

I shrugged. "Sort of. This year is so much greater though because I got the best Christmas present of all."

She gave me a weird look and her eyes darted back to our empty, pitiful little tree. "You didn't get anything," she said. "I literally left your gifts in Collier under the tree at the Alpha house without even thinking."

I shrugged again. "I got you, Sport. What more could I possibly want or need?"

She smiled happily and kissed me.

An alarm started alerting in the kitchen. I ran to investigate and found the entire room filled with smoke. It was only then that I remembered the cinnamon rolls in the oven.

"Oh no!" Shelby cried. "I ruined our first Christmas breakfast."

We opened the windows to air the place out. Fortunately, even with a dusting of snow on the ground, our wolves would help regulate our temperatures and keep us warm.

To console her I carried her back to the bedroom, the furthest point away from the smoke. Three hours later we'd successfully christened all the main rooms of the house and were late for Christmas brunch at Maddie and Liam's. When we walked in and Maddie asked if everything was okay, I couldn't wipe the grin off my face.

"Gross," Maddie said, rolling her eyes.

"I didn't say a word," I insisted.

"You don't have to. You two reek of sex, and burnt cinnamon," Liam whispered. Shelby's face turned several shades of red. "You sure you don't want to bail on this?"

I laughed. "We're sure. I could use the break anyway before she wears me out," I said, waggling my eyebrows up and down at Shelby. She smacked me across my stomach and went to help Maddie in the kitchen. I refrained from issuing a warning against that.

"If we'd had more notice, I would have at least stocked some basics. Did you sleep on the floor last night?"

"Nah, we stopped for the priorities. You know, air mattress, coffee pot, and the ugliest Christmas tree ever."

Liam laughed. "You definitely have your priorities, I see."

Christmas day was nice. Liam gave me a couple of camp chairs to take back with us and Maddie sent us home with enough food for a few days. Later in the evening, it felt like each person in Westin pack stopped in to say hello and Merry Christmas. Every single one of them brought food for us, too. It was a nice gesture and truly made us feel welcome to the territory.

I looked in our now over-stuffed refrigerator and laughed. "I'm not sure we're going to need to shop for food for a month."

"It's been an interesting day, that's for sure," Shelby said as she hugged me.

Yet another knock on the door interrupted our first moment of quiet together.

Shelby groaned before planting a smile on her face and going to answer the door. "It's Patrick," she yelled back a few seconds later.

"I'm diving into a pie. You want a slice?" I hollered back.

Shelby walked into the kitchen with more than just Patrick. Elise was with him as was a large, menacing looking man I had never met before.

"Oops, sorry. I thought it was just Patrick. Hi, Benjamin Shay," I said, setting the pie aside and offering the guy my hand.

"Silas Granger."

Of course I recognized the name. "Oh, I didn't think we'd be meeting for a few days still," I said honestly.

"We have a situation that requires immediate attention. Our team is leaving first thing in the morning. I'm aware we haven't even begun onboarding yet, but I'm also aware this is only a trial. If you'd like to tag along, the invite stands. I know you and your mate just arrived, so if you need the next few days to settle in, that's okay too," he said.

Something about the way he emphasized "mate" told me he was not at all thrilled about me having attachments. I could appreciate that, but also knew I'd have to work that much harder to prove myself to him.

My eyes darted to Shelby, who nodded subtly.
"What time do we leave?" I asked.
Silas smirked. "Zero four hundred."
"I'll be ready," I assured him.
"Great," Patrick said. "Now, how about that pie."

Ben

Chapter 25

I felt bad leaving Shelby so soon after our arrival, but there was no way I could turn down the job. I knew that I was being scrutinized every second I was with the team.

They hadn't given me any information about the mission or where we were meeting. Patrick had not given me a tour of the place yet, but he had told me enough that I had recognized the lodge they operated out of on our drive in. So, at three-thirty the next morning, I pulled up to the lodge and investigated for signs of movement.

It didn't take long for me to find what I was looking for. Two jeeps at the back of the property were being loaded and Silas was easy to spot amongst them.

I knew from the way he looked down at his watch and from the frustrated vibes he was giving off that the invitation for me to tag along had been Patrick's idea. Silas had clearly been planning on ditching me.

"Good morning," I said.

"I see you made it. Patrick give you directions?" Silas asked.

I snorted. "No. You guys purposely left that part vague enough, but I've been doing this shit a long time. I know my way around a mission."

I didn't know what I would be needing on the trip, so I had packed my general gear bag that contained everything I could possibly need. If the army had done anything for me, it was to assert the need to always be prepared.

"This the temp?" someone asked. I looked up to see a guy walking towards me. Silas was a big dude, but this man was huge. His ripped arms were easily the size of tree trunks.

"Benjamin Shay," I said, offering him my hand.

"Painter," he replied. "This is Grant, Tucker, and Elliot," he said, introducing the rest of the team. They all stopped what they were doing just long enough to give a head nod of acknowledgement without saying a word before returning to their preparations.

Silas appeared pissed that I made it, so I stayed out of their way and just evaluated things. I was surprised to find such a small unit and wanted to ask if that was the full team or only a partial, but I didn't dare.

When we loaded up, I chose to join the jeep Painter was driving and give Silas some space. I knew how protective Crawley had always been of us and how hesitant he was to take on new people. I couldn't imagine how much hell he'd give to someone like me insisting on a trial before joining his team. It was necessary for Shelby, but I knew it was going to make my life hell until a final decision was made.

We drove to the airport where a plane was waiting. I wanted to groan. I hadn't considered the mission would be that far away. I had a million questions to ask, but I opted to keep my head down and my mouth shut instead.

Once settled in for the flight, the guys turned to me with questions.

"I know Silas was forced into this arrangement by Patrick. He's none too happy about it. My question is, what the hell do you have on Patrick O'Connell to get him to agree to a damn trial? 'Cause that's not how we function around here. You're either in or you're not," Painter said.

"I don't have anything on Patrick," I said honestly. "And I get it. I don't particularly like it either, but I made the mistake of signing my life away to the military for nine years and I'm not about to blindly sign on for anything like that again."

"No way he'd just agree to a trial, not in this unit. Must be something good to convince Silas to play along," he insisted.

"That's enough, Painter," Silas barked.

"With all due respect, we don't function well with secrets in this unit, Silas, and you damn well know it. I don't need to be looking over my shoulder keeping an eye on the temp instead of the target," he insisted.

Silas glared at me and it dawned on me, he really didn't know.

I sighed. "Verndari truth serum."

"What?" Silas and Painter asked in unison.

"That's the price I negotiated to get this trial," I told them honestly. "Despite how it appears. I am a team player and I know the importance of trust and honesty. I don't expect you to just take my word on that. I'll do my part to prove myself no matter how much shit you throw at me."

"How the hell did you get your hands on Verndari truth serum?" Silas asked.

I shrugged. "Might not have anything on Patrick O'Connell, but I had enough on some higher up officers to make it happen."

"You're telling me the U.S. military is using goddamn truth serum now?" Silas cursed.

I nodded. "Only on rare occasions, but yeah, they're experimenting with it."

"Jesus Christ. It's bad enough we have to monitor the Verndari using that stuff, but now the military too?" Painter questioned.

"This is nuts," Grant said.

"What do we do with this information?" Elliot asked.

"Am I the only one that thinks it's funny that everyone takes the temp's word for this so easily?" Tucker laughed.

I shrugged. "Take my word on it, or don't; it's up to you. I've been through more than my fair share of hazing already, and I'm getting too old for that bullshit. You have questions for me, ask them."

"If you're such a team player, why did you really ask for a trial period?" Tucker asked.

I smiled. "To give my mate time to adjust," I told them honestly.

"Shit! You're mated?" Painter asked.

"Yeah I am, and I would have been nine years ago if I hadn't been a hotheaded dumbass who jumped the gun and joined the military. I lost nine years with her, and I'm not going to make that mistake again. I know damn well that there aren't many opportunities for an ex-sniper and I'm lucky to get this chance, but I need it to be right for Shelby, too."

"How much of that shit did you give O'Connell for him to not only agree to the trial but to offer it to a mated guy?" Elliot said.

I laughed. "Being mated had nothing to do with it. Not sure how many of you are wolves," I said.

"None," Painter said.

"Really?"

"Really," Silas confirmed.

"Okay, well you had to have learned something about wolves working so closely with Westin Pack, right?"

"Sure," he said.

"Okay, well, Westin has certain packs they are closely aligned with."

"Longhorn, Alaska, New York, and Collier being the top four," Tucker told me.

"Right, so my mate is a Collier wolf," I said.

They stared at me like, "So?"

"You're a Collier wolf, so that's not all that surprising," Silas said.

"Yes, but I mean she's actual Collier. Shelby Collier, fifth daughter of Zach Collier. Her family is really close to the Westins. Patrick probably wouldn't have given me the time of day otherwise," I admitted.

"That makes a little more sense," Painter conceded.

"I still don't like it," Silas grumbled.

I nodded. "Crawley wouldn't either. He told me you and he worked together on a few joint missions during your military years."

"Hey, how the hell do you know Crawley?" Silas asked.

I gave a sad smile. "He's the leader of the Ghosts, or what's left of them at least."

"The Ghosts?" Grant asked. "What the hell do you know about the Ghosts?"

"Oh yeah, that was the other part of my deal with Patrick. I hear you want to recruit from them. I have the contacts you need for that."

"Crawley's leading the goddamn Ghosts now? How did I not know that?" Silas barked.

I grinned. "We're Ghosts—we don't actually exist."

Under normal circumstances I would never have divulged this information, but this was my team now and, in my experience, secrets got people killed.

By the time our plane landed there was less hostility towards me, but I knew I would still need to prove myself.

"No briefing?" I asked when the door opened.

Elliot snorted. "We were briefed yesterday."

"Great," I said, following them out.

"Temp, you're going to be Painter's problem today," Silas ordered. "Tucker, you too. Elliot and Grant, you're with me."

When each of the guys pulled out their weapons, I moved to reach for my own.

"Give the temp a gun," Silas finally said.

"No need, I prefer my own," I said pulling out a pistol to strap to my waist.

The guys laughed when they saw my pistol and proceeded to hand me an AK-47. I waved them off and piece by piece I pulled my own out of my bag and reassembled.

"Is that fully automatic?" Painter asked.

I grinned. "It's capable of it if I choose it to be."

"You had all that in your backpack?" Tucker asked. "Damn, I thought I was good at packing toys."

I didn't tell them I had two barrels and a scope still in there that I could mod my baby into a makeshift long gun in a pinch. It wasn't as good as my queen back home as a sniper gun, but it would do in an emergency.

"A team, let's roll out," Silas said as Grant and Elliot followed him out of the plane.

I wanted to press for instructions or at least have some inkling of what the mission was, but I got the feeling it was a test and being withheld deliberately.

"Let's go," Painter finally said.

On the tarmac there was a black SUV waiting for us. Tucker drove. Painter took the passenger seat, so I hopped into the back.

"Tell him, Painter. Please. We need the backup if something goes wrong."

"Silas's orders, Tucker. He's only here to observe."

"Then why the hell is he packing more heat than we are?"

Painter laughed. "He was supposed to be issued a gun with blanks."

"And this is why I prefer to use my own. How the hell am I supposed to trust you guys if you pull something like that on an actual mission?" I asked.

"We're more concerned with how the hell we're supposed to trust you," Painter told me.

"I have been completely forthcoming with you," I reminded him. "I didn't have to tell you guys any of that stuff. It was between me and O'Connell."

"He's right," Tucker said. "Tell him."

"Christ, fine, but we're only backup on this mission. We sit back and let Silas handle this. That's why there was no concern with giving you blanks," Painter said. "I know you're aware of the Verndari, but do you know who the Raglan are?"

"The rogue unit of the Verndari," I said. "I'm aware."

"We've been tracking them and taking down one cell after another. More often than not they get tipped off and move before we get there, but last fall we took down a major cell at Archibald Reynolds College and scored hundreds of boxes of data," Painter said.

"Shit! They're at the shifter college?" I asked. I was struggling to believe what they were saying.

"Yup, it was bad. From the documentation we found there, we identified several other locations they operate out of, but of course they all went dark. We've been laying low, but our intel says there's activity at this location again. We have to move fast if that's the case. Silas is going in and confirming, while we're on standby, along with three other units just in case."

Tucker pulled into a parking lot near the site. "So basically, we sit here and wait," he said.

Twenty minutes passed. Tucker fell asleep and Painter thumbed through the same magazine for the fifth time. I had been on my fair share of stakeouts, but this one I was not prepared for. My wolf was getting restless being cooped up in the car, but I didn't dare complain.

A large boom was heard close enough to rattle our vehicle. Everyone sprang into action.

"Shit! What the hell did Elliot do this time? Ears in," Painter yelled, passing earpieces to each of us.

"Cover the rear exit," Silas barked through the earpiece.

"Which building?" I asked calmly.

"To our one o'clock, Tucker told me."

As they exited the car and began sweeping the area heading towards the rear exit, I hung back just enough to cover their asses. My gun was to the ready as I looked high and low for any signs of trouble.

"Run," I yelled, seeing movement on the partially collapsed building and the glimmer of light off a rifle. "Sniper on the roof."

Bullets rained down, targeting Tucker and Painter. I stayed behind and waited for my shot. One bullet was all I needed when my opportunity came.

"Sniper terminated," I informed them before walking to the door.

Tucker waited just inside the door while Painter scouted ahead.

"Thanks, man," he said. "You really had our backs back there."

"That's my job," I reminded him. "Come on."

We caught up to Painter. It had been radio silent since I alerted them to the sniper.

"What's going on?" Tucker whispered to him.

Painter signaled for us to be quiet and get down. Instead, I moved into a safe position to cover them both.

"Delta is in position."

"Gamma in position."

"Charlie has eyes in the sky."

Painter motioned for us to move.

The wing we were in appeared to be deserted, but the closer we got to the collapsed section, the more signs we saw of recent activity.

Finally, at the end of a hallway, just before the collapse, we stumbled into a lab that wasn't entirely abandoned.

"Blood," I said as we entered the room.

There were cages lining one wall with people in them.

"You're safe now," Painter told them as Tucker ran to open the cages.

With the prisoners free, Tucker sat down at a computer and began hacking into their system for any information he could find.

My eyes darted around the room and over each of the prisoners.

"Where's the damn blood coming from?" I finally asked. My sensitive wolf nose had picked it up before we even entered the room.

A teenage boy, white with fright, slowly pointed to a table near the collapsed side of the room. I quickly realized this room had been significantly larger before the collapse. What had we done?

I heard a moan and moved in to investigate. On a table, partially buried in debris, was a woman. She was gasping for breath and grabbed my arm when I got close. She was shaking uncontrollably and when she opened her mouth to speak, blood trickled out.

"Painter, Tucker, over here," I yelled. "Help me get her out."

We worked together to pull her our of the pile of collapsed ceiling on top of her. It was there that I found the problem. She was very large with child and her pants were soaked in blood.

"Please," she said, grabbing my arm and staring into my eyes. With her last breath, she took my hand and placed it on her stomach.

When I felt the baby inside her move, I knew I couldn't leave without at least trying to save it.

"Leave it, Ben. She's gone," Painter said.

"Maybe, but we might be able to save the baby."

With a newfound determination, I quickly rounded up the necessary supplies. Several of the prisoners jumped in to help when they realized what I was about to attempt. I was no medic, but from previous experience in the field, this wasn't going to be my first C-section.

"Alcohol," someone said, thrusting it into my hand.

"Scalpel," another person said.

"Here's a stack of clean towels."

Painter shook his head. "If you're going to do this, you have to move fast, and we need to get the hell out of here."

I nodded.

Taking a deep breath, I began making the incision. It was gruesome and blood was everywhere, but I managed to make the necessary cut to expose the baby. I reached in and pulled out a baby girl. There were tears in my eyes when she cried and took her first breath.

"It's a girl!" Tucker yelled as I handed the baby off to a woman with a clean towel, waiting with open arms.

I cut the umbilical cord, and everyone was moving quickly towards the door. I wasn't sure what possessed me to turn back to the woman, but I did, and snapped a quick picture on my phone. It was then that I noticed movement within her womb.

"Hold up," I said.

I reached back in and pulled out another baby. It was a boy, and he was holding the hand of yet another.

"Shit! There's two more. Someone grab some more clean towels."

There was no way I was leaving these babies behind.

I delivered a second baby boy and triple checked to make certain there weren't any more.

"Triplets?" Tucker said. "Bloody hell, this is the craziest assignment I've ever been on."

He took the first boy, while I held on to the last. With their umbilical cords cut, and safely wrapped in clean towels, we made our way back out of the building.

Silas had given the all clear during the births and Delta and Gamma teams were moving in to search for any information or further survivors.

Once outside, the woman handed the baby girl to me. "I don't know much," she said. "The mother was a wolf shifter from New York Pack. They were experimenting on her the last three days. That is all I know."

"Thank you," I said.

"Thank you for saving us." She smiled down at the two babies in my arms. "All of us."

I quickly found Silas in the chaos. "These newborns need immediate treatment."

He looked me over and sighed. "Grant. Take the second car and get the temp and these kids to safety. We're close to the New

York Pack. The Alpha there may let you have access to his pack physician."

Tucker passed the second baby off to Grant and we ran to the car I'd arrived in. I lined the babies on the floorboard and sat in the backseat with them.

Grant got on the phone to get clearance for us to enter New York territory. The Alpha met us at the designation he gave us, with his pack physician in tow.

"Do we even know what kind of shifters they are?" he asked me while the doctor checked the babies over.

"Wolves. One of yours if the prisoner there was correct." I pulled out my phone and pulled up the picture I'd taken of the woman.

"Shit! That's Alice."

"One of yours?"

"Yeah," he confirmed.

"Great, then I'm sure you already know who the father is and can pass the pups off to him," I said.

"Actually, I don't. Alice wasn't mated. She went missing only five months ago though, and these are full-term babies, or pretty close. I'll send word through the Pack and see if we can identify him."

"Thanks. I'd appreciate that."

"Heard you were the one who personally delivered them."

I nodded. "Yeah. I just couldn't leave them there," I confessed.

Four hours later the babies were clean and determined healthy, but there had been no leads on the father. Worse, news had spread that Alice had been taken by the Raglans and because the rumors told people that they were experimenting on shifters, no one in New York Pack would step up and take them, not even the Alpha.

"Honestly, Ben, I can't. I've put out calls to the five closest packs to see if anyone will take three newborns. I've had offers to take the girl by two families, but no one so far willing to take all three," he told me. "I'll find someone to look after them for a few days, but if nothing better arises, I'll pass off the girl and call the human authorities to take the boys. I'm sorry. I know you went through a lot to save them, but that's the best I can do."

I was torn up inside and didn't know how to proceed.

"I'm sorry, man," Grant said. "Too bad you and your mate can't just take them."

I froze and stared at him. "What did you say?"

"I said, it's a shame you can't just take them. You're already attached to them and risked a lot to bring them into this world."

I sat down hard on the ground and ran my hands through my hair. "Alpha? Would that be an option?"

"What? For you to take them?" he asked.

I nodded. "Yes, my mate and I. Of course I'd have to clear that with her first, but would you agree to that?"

"What animal spirit are you, Ben?" he asked.

"Wolf sir, from Collier Pack, though we reside currently in Westin territory."

"Let me put in some calls to Thomas and Kyle. I need to let them know the fears my people have and make certain they are okay with that."

"May I ask what fears?"

"If Alice was with the Raglans the entire time she was gone, who knows what sort of experiments she was subjected to. They're calling the babies 'freaks of nature' that shouldn't be alive."

I growled. "They're just babies, for goddamn sake."

He smiled sadly. "I agree with you, but my pack has been hit harder than most by the Raglans especially over the last year. There's a lot of fear right now, which is why I think it would be in their best interest not to be raised in my territory."

He made some phone calls and came back with a smile on his face. "Talk to your mate, Ben. If she's willing to take them, all three are yours."

I sucked in a deep breath and nodded.

My hand was shaking when I reached for my phone and dialed Shelby's number.

"Hey, handsome. How'd your first day of work go? Are you back?" she asked.

"No, um, I've been delayed. Sport, I need you to sit down," I said.

"Ben, you're freaking me out. What's wrong?"

"Um, nothing. Nothing's wrong, but I did something today and it could turn out to be life-changing for us. I hate to spring this on you, but I need an immediate and final answer."

"What is it?"

"Today's mission didn't go quite as planned," I started. "A bomb went off and it caused a partial collapse. There were still people inside, and one of them was very pregnant."

"Oh my gosh. Is she okay?"

"No, she died, but I delivered her babies, Shelbs."

"Wow, that's incredible, Ben."

"It was. Triplets! Their mother was a wolf shifter and there is nothing known about their father. She was suspected to have been with some pretty bad people for the last five months and possibly experimented on in ways we may never understand."

"That's horrible," she cried.

I smiled. "Their Pack can't take them, Shelbs and the best we've come up with so far is to send the girl to one home and the boys to foster care."

"What? You can't do that. They're shifters, Ben. You can't put them into the human system."

"I agree, which is why you have roughly five minutes to tell me if I'm walking away or bringing them home forever."

"Are you saying what I think you're saying?" she asked.

I hung up and immediately called her back through video chat.

"Benjamin, I cannot believe you just hung up on me."

I laughed. "I just needed to see your face for this. You know we've always talked about having a big family. This could be the opportunity to make that dream come true."

She sucked in a deep breath and tears streamed down her cheeks. "Are you worried about those things you mentioned?"

I shook my head. "No, and we'll cross that bridge if it ever comes up that we need to worry."

"Is this really happening?" she asked.

I hit the button to flip the camera around as the doctor and Tucker held the babies. I zoomed in on each of them.

"You tell me, Sport?"

Shelby was crying openly now but smiling through her tears. "You bring those sweet babies home, Benjamin Shay."

"Yes, ma'am," I said, feeling happier than I ever knew possible.

Shelby

Epilogue

Being a first-time mom was hard. Being a first-time mom of triplets was complete insanity. I wasn't sure I was ever going to sleep again, but it was all worth it.

It took a few days for Ben to work out the legalities and paperwork for the babies. They finally all arrived home, safe and sound on New Year's Eve.

Of course I had the nursery complete and the house filled and babyproofed before their arrival. Peyton and Clara had flown in to help me and Maddie and Kelsey had supplied massive amounts of hand-me-downs.

Still, no amount of planning could have prepared me for the first moment I held my children in my arms. That was one month ago today. It's crazy how much life can change in a few short months.

I went from being lonely and single, pining for a life I never thought I could have, to being a mate and a mother. The triplets could never replace my little Annabelle Grace, but my heart was big enough to love them just as much.

Nathan Don, Zachary Thomas, and Mary Alice were my whole world. Okay, their daddy held a huge part of it, too.

Silas was still giving Ben shit for his trial period and insisted on calling him "Temp" even though he had signed on full-time a week ago. Bravo company was exactly what Ben had needed, and he had proven himself to them quickly. Each mission he left for still made me nervous, but I supposed that was just normal life for the mate of a hero.

I looked down at Mary Alice asleep in my arms and kissed her sweet head and smiled. Begrudgingly I got up and laid her down in her crib, and then froze. I looked across the room expecting to hear crying, but it was silent.

I slowly backed out of the room, not daring enough to close the door entirely for fear the click of the latch would wake one of them.

I ran down the hall and jumped into bed triumphantly.

Ben laughed. "What is that all about?"

"Listen," I said.

He frowned. "I don't hear anything."

"I know, because all three of them are asleep at a normal hour for probably the first time in their entire lives."

He laughed and high fived me, then pulled me close and kissed me. Juggling three newborns meant very little alone time for mommy and daddy. I quietly got back out of bed and shut the door to our bedroom, holding my breath the entire time.

I double checked the charge on the video monitors, and turned the volume up, before I turned the dampener on.

"Wait. Does this mean what I think it means?" Ben asked, as he leapt from the bed and tore off his PJs in record time.

I sighed happily, staring at my gorgeous mate. My sex clenched with desire as I pulled my shirt over my head and dropped it down onto the floor.

He rounded the bed and growled as he approached me.

"Sorry, Sport, no time for foreplay. Last time I came this close to having you, Mary Alice put an abrupt end to it."

I giggled as I wrapped my arms around him and let him have his way with me. After a few quick kisses, he turned me around and bent me over the bed. His body melted against mine as he took me from behind fast and furiously until I screamed out his name and collapsed onto the mattress.

Feeling satiated, we climbed back into the bed. Ben smiled down at me with a twinkle in his eye.

"Now we can make time for foreplay," he said as his mouth found my left breast and flicked his tongue across my nipple.

My body was still on fire, and my nerves raw. I moaned at the sensations beginning to stir within me.

Suddenly, a loud wail came through the monitors. We both froze and waited to see if it was just a one-time occurrence. No such luck.

I looked at the monitors and picked up baby three. "Nathan," I sighed.

Ben gave me one more kiss before climbing out of bed and retrieving his pajama bottoms.

"My turn," he said.

"Are you sure? I really don't mind."

He winked at me. "You relax. I'm going to bribe him to go right back to sleep, but from now on, quickies are definitely the way to go."

I giggled as he leaned down and planted one last kiss on my lips before heading for the nursery. I watched him on the monitor as he picked up his son and cuddled him close to his naked chest.

"Listen, little man. We need to talk. Tonight is mommy and daddy time, so I'm going to need you to go back to sleep."

I smiled, my heart overflowing with joy. I was an exhausted, overly emotional new mom, mated to my best friend in the whole world. I knew there was nothing in life we couldn't overcome together.

I felt pretty damn lucky. No, my life wasn't easy, and it was far from perfect, but it was all mine, and I was finally living my very own happily ever after.

Dear Reader,

Welp, that's the end of another series. I know some of you will be sad to say goodbye to Collier Pack, but I hope you enjoyed Shelby and Ben's story. If you did, please consider leaving a review at https://mybook.to/Collier5

You may be wondering what comes next? Well… **WESTIN FORCE** will kick off in 2020!!! I am super excited to share the sexy alpha males of Bravo company with you all in a paramilitary addition to the Westin World. Stalkers links below will keep you informed on the release schedule and what to expect to come. There are still several ARC Shifter books on the horizon too, so be on the lookout for exciting news to come!

For further information on my books, events, and life in general, I can be found online here:

Website: http://www.julietrettel.com

Facebook: http://www.facebook.com/authorjulietrettel

Facebook Fan Group: https://www.facebook.com/groups/compounderspod7/

Instagram: http://www.instagram.com/julie.trettel

Twitter: http://www.twitter.com/julietrettel

Goodreads: http://www.goodreads.com/author/show/14703924.Julie_Trettel

BookBub: https://www.bookbub.com/authors/julie-trettel

Amazon: http://www.amazon.com/Julie_Trettel/e/B018HS9GXS

Join my newsletter! http://eepurl.com/cwRHij

Much love and thanks,
Julie Trettel

Check out more great books by Julie Trettel!

The Compounders Series

The Compounders: Book1
https://mybook.to/Compounders1

DISSENSION
https://mybook.to/Compounders2

DISCONTENT
https://mybook.to/CompoundersNovella

SEDITION
https://mybook.to/Compounders3

Westin Pack

One True Mate
https://mybook.to/Westin1

Fighting Destiny
https://mybook.to/Westin2

Forever Mine
https://mybook.to/Westin3

Confusing Hearts
https://mybook.to/Westin4

Can't Be Love
https://mybook.to/Westin5

Under a Harvest Moon

https://mybook.to/WestinPrequel

Collier Pack

Breathe Again
https://mybook.to/Collier1

Run Free
https://mybook.to/Collier2

In Plain Sight
https://mybook.to/Collier3

Broken Chains
https://mybook.to/Collier4

ARC Shifters

Pack's Promise
https://mybook.to/PacksPromise

Winter's Promise
https://mybook.to/ARC2

Midnight Promise
https://mybook.to/MidnightPromise

Stones of Amaria

Legends of Sorcery
https://mybook.to/LegendsOfSorcery

Ruins of Magic
https://mybook.to/RuinsofMagic

About the Author

Julie Trettel is author of The Compounders, Westin Pack, Collier Pack, and ARC Shifters Series. She comes from a long line of story tellers. Writing has always been a stress reliever and escape for her to manage the crazy demands of juggling time and schedules between work and an active family of six. In her "free time," she enjoys traveling, reading, outdoor activities, and spending time with family and friends.

Visit

www.JulieTrettel.com

Made in the USA
Las Vegas, NV
27 April 2022